Buffalo Morgan's Kinglomafux

Sick & Funny Comedy from Buffalo's Vegas Show

Barry Hemmerle

Editing by Amy Lignor

Book 4

DEDICATION

This book is dedicated to everybody with something to say who can express it through whatever artistic form they choose.

I also want to give a great deal of credit to my son, Dan. His opinions of my writing help keep me focused on making my books as entertaining as possible.

I'm also bringing a new illustrator into the Morgan family. Dillon Gilligan is a true friend and a real talent with a wonderful imagination. Thank you, Dillon!

Also...a big "HELLO" goes out to my first grandchild, Jason Hemmerle. You are most definitely allowed to read this...when you turn 30.

Buffalo Morgan's King Lomafux

Sick & Funny Comedy from Buffalo's Vegas
Show
By Barry Hemmerle

For more books like this one, visit Barry Hemmerle's
website at:
http://barryhemmerle.com/

Printed in the United States of America
The publisher offers discounts on this book when
ordered in bulk quantities. For more information,
contact Sales Department, Phone 815-290-9605,
Email:
sales@FreedomOfSpeechPublishing.com

Freedom of Speech Publishing, Leawood KS, 66224
www.FreedomOfSpeechPublishing.com

ISBN: 1-938634-16-0
ISBN-13: 978-1-938634-16-1

A SPECIAL THANK YOU TO YOU!

On behalf of everyone at Freedom Of Speech Publishing, thank you for choosing Buffalo Morgan's King Lomafux: Sick & Funny Comedy from Buffalo's Vegas Show for your reading enjoyment.

As an added bonus and special thank you, for purchasing Buffalo Morgan's King Lomafux: Sick & Funny Comedy from Buffalo's Vegas Show, you can enjoy discounts and special promotions on other Freedom of Speech Publishing products. Visit http://freedomofspeechpublishing.com/vip/ to learn more.

We are committed to providing you with the highest level of customer satisfaction possible. If for any reason you have questions or comments, we are delighted to hear from you. Email us at cs@freedomofspeechpublishing.com or visit our website at: http://freedomofspeechpublishing.com/contact-us-2/.

If you enjoyed Buffalo Morgan's King Lomafux: Sick & Funny Comedy from Buffalo's Vegas Show, visit www.freedomofspeechpublishing.com for a list of similar books or upcoming books.

Again, thank you for your patronage. We look forward to providing you more entertainment in the future.

ACKNOWLEDGMENTS

I'd like to thank my son, Dan, for banging out my chicken scratch into a readable art form.

Chasity for the great artwork in the book.

My editor, Amy, who lives in a desert for some reason or another. As long as I mention Mötley Crüe in my book somewhere, she likes my stuff.

And Pat, my publisher. He and his staff go a long way to make my books the pieces of art they eventually become.

Lastly, Dillon Gilligan, my friend. He also helped me out with the artwork in the book.

Thank you all.

"A man doesn't become a king without a strong army behind him."

Thank you, EVERYBODY...

Introduction

Any stand-up comic will tell you that some of their best material came from ad-libbing some other bit. That is all this book is…

When I perform and am standing in the first couple minutes on stage, if I feel the audience is loving my show, I'll abandon my "standard" act and just ad-lib bits. Just say anything that rolls into my head.

And if it did really well, I'd try to remember it and write it down when I got off stage. One time, as I was leaving the stage, I could feel this one bit that really killed was slipping out of my mind.

Well, this couple came up to me with paper and pen in hand for an autograph. I grabbed it, and within 10 seconds I wrote down enough of the bit to remember for later. Then I signed it and made a Xerox copy, handing them the original. What…? What's a Xerox? (It came between the Pony Express and the cell phone!)

So this is a book of stories I remember telling. No segues. No chapters. One wacky story crashing into the next.

Enjoy!

I'd just like to point out one of the unsung heroes of the "household products" industry. I don't have any idea how anybody survived in the ancient world without this incredible invention. I can't imagine my life without it.

So how about a big round of applause for one of all our favorites...toilet paper. I love toilet paper. I have an irrational fear that someday we'll run out. Every time our country finds itself in another world conflict, I find myself in one of those megalo-crap stores.

I'll tap some guy wearing a tard vest on the shoulder: "Excuse me, sir, can you find me a forklift and take my skid of 2-ply to my rented van right there? Ok, thanks buddy."

———

You might think of a derelict as a waste of human life over 50 years old. Truth is, there are young derelicts. I guess you can call them "Derelict saplings."

Every little cliché has one. Look at the Beatles. Their sapling was Ringo. And as a mating partner, you kind of have to find your "equivalent." They do not come out of the woodwork, mind you. You theoretically stand on a street corner and announce your short comings, pause, and then hope a mate is on an adjacent street with the same level of social or physical deformity.

Our "sapling" would probably still be a virgin if he didn't find a hundred dollar bill at our bus stop. And no, he didn't slice a hole in Ben Franklin's head and stick his pinga in it. Well…maybe he did. The guy at the liquor store did seem pretty pissed off when he handed it to him.

But you probably already know what I'm going to say. He bought a fifth of Jack and a gram of coke. And then he used it as bait to get laid. I mean, I would have done the same thing, but I would have gotten better nibbles than he did. The princess he reeled in was 90 pounds bigger than him. She sucked up all his blow in one snort, then knocked him out in one punch because he was out of coke.

To show she had a heart, however, while he was unconscious on the ground, she kicked him really hard in the cookies. I think her feeling was when he woke up, he would think that agonizing pain was from sex…and he did. And he bragged about it. And we all told him we were there. We saw it all.

She kicked you in the balls because she did not want you to reproduce…ever. She said, "The next generation of your family tree will be a bunch of sticks."

And she was so happy after she did it, you'd have thought she saved the world from a future pestilence. Then she just picked up your bottle of Jack and walked off.

And when we got done laughing at you and spitting nasty insults at you, we left you to die in the mud. The next day, you came around acting like nothing happened. And that is why you are our "derelict sapling."

Here's a typical story about this dude:

I threw a wild alcohol party when we were 17, hanging out at a lake.

So, as the host, I'm circulating around and come up on this misfit. He's leaning up on a tree, puking on himself. So I asked him, "Do you always puke on yourself?"

He looked me right in the eye, and said: "No, not all the time."

———

I love how people get so sucked up in fashion. Somebody says something like "this is great" or "that is" and people will stampede to the stores—checkbooks in hand—to have it.

An example... Ugg Boots. If these boots are named after someone, it must be some dude from 100 centuries ago. There was probably only about 10 names back then. The doctor hands the baby to its mother, and asks, "What you name it, Mrs. Lee?"

"Me call it, Ugg."

You never know. It may have been some modern day schmuck. "Hey, let's fuck with our kid from day one."

But getting back to the boots… They look and feel like high-top slippers. And they have little white fluff balls coming out of the top. Is this supposed to be an abstract illusion of your feet being so comfy that it's like wearing little sacks of fresh cotton on your feet? And, talk about expensive cotton!

They're like $200…and they're not even steel toed.

———

I know a lot of you ladies have figured it out, but for those of you that are a little slow in the head, I'm going to reveal a little secret to you about how to get your man to do almost anything you want them to do. And I say "almost," because there's certain things we will not do.

That usually involves us doing something hazardous with our pingas.

We will not prove our love for you by sticking our pingas in a blender…unless it's unplugged. Although I don't see why either situation should turn up.

We will not use our pingas to check an electrical oven even though you said the power breaker was off.

I'm sure the words, "Are you sure you hit the right breaker?" were the famous last words of a few fun-loving, yet stupid men.

And if you get mad at us and it can't be resolved by bedtime, I say we can go to bed mad. However, in my case, I would be wearing my aluminum underwear and sleeping on my stomach.

Ok, back to getting your husband or boyfriend to do stuff. The secret is... oh shit, hold on. I forgot...oh wait...ok, uh...let him get liquored up first. That's it. With that...deals can be struck.

If I'm going to spend Saturday walking the mall with you, going from shoe store to freaking shoe store, giving my opinion that you constantly ask me for only to be dragged back and forth 6 times because you can't decide whether you want burgundy or sunset colored shoes, I want to be loaded.

Let me walk around with a travel mug full of scotch and you can walk me to hell and back.

I just want a steady buzz, then you can showcase the whole store to me. Everything will be fine as long as I don't breathe on anyone.

And the buzz thing isn't just for the malls. (Guys, if you like records, I once found and paid for a pair of shoes in under 53 seconds. Women don't understand those kinds of records, but you will.)

Anyway…yeah, the booze thing works for visiting with her kin, too.

"Honey, we're having dinner over at my parents tonight."

"Ok, let me just fill up my little sippy cup and we'll be on our way."

If you follow my philosophy, keep your altitude at a controllable level. Don't embarrass yourself. Don't be "that guy."

Don't giggle at a funeral. Some people consider that "politically incorrect." And when you say your final goodbye, don't say something stupid like, "Thanks for dying, Uncle James. It's been a long time since I've been to an open bar." If you want to think it, go ahead. But don't make it audible. Don't even mouth it. There's always someone there who can read lips.

Don't go to weddings to get bombed, either…you know, unless you're the groom. Then "glug, glug."

Last thing you want is to be "out of your mind" and bragging about banging the bride, especially when everybody knows she's one of your close family members. Now those types of rumors take forever to die down. Like…decades. And no, that wasn't me.

See, sometimes I have to explain these things; I've had my fans come up and ask me if my jokes are actual life experiences. A lot of them are.

This couple last week asked me if my McDonalds bit was real and I said, "Yeah, more or less." Then the woman leans in towards me and asks about the 3 guys and the watermelon. Then she asked if I was one of those guys. I just kind of looked through her. "You're really asking me if I banged a watermelon? I worked in McDonalds' in probably 70% of the United States. No, I didn't bang a watermelon."

This was the perfect couple to hit them with an "oldie but goodie" joke. So I asked them, "Do you want to hear a joke?"

And they were both standing there with big ole dumbass smiles, "Yeah, this is great."

So I said, "How do you keep a moron in suspense?" Then I walked away to get a fresh beer. Seconds later, they're following me through a roomful of people to the kitchen.

"Come on dude, finish the joke. You can't leave us hanging like this."

Actually...I can. 45 minutes to be exact. They almost had me twice. Both times I went to the bathroom. I know they were camped right outside the door, so I climbed out the window. Then I would show up in another part of the house.

After a while, I just got tired of dodging them. So...I left, fuck 'em. Thinking I banged a watermelon...?? They didn't exactly deserve politeness.

————

I probably would not do too well in jail. I think I would never catch on to the prison lingo. If I'm in the rec hall and some big dude walks up to me and starts talking, I don't want to misunderstand.

Con: "Hey you? Boy! After dinner I'm having some wonderful dessert. Do you want to guess what I'm having? I'll give you a hint... You're sitting on it."

Me: "You're gonna eat this bench?"

Con: "No boy, I'm talking about sex."

Me: "You're gonna have sex with this bench?" Oh god, maybe that wasn't mashed potatoes I sat in.

Con: "Oh no, boy, I'm talking about you."

Me: "Dude, I'm not having sex with a bench."

Con: "Are you really this stupid, boy? Me and you are having sex after dinner tonight. Do you understand that?"

Me: "Well first off, I believe it's "you and I." Second, you assume too much. You're assuming I have nothing to do tonight. I have a life. And you're assuming I'm gay, which I'm not. And even if I was, I doubt I could get hard looking at your fat, pock-marked, zit encrusted, rats nest of an ass. And I'm sure as hell not letting you on my back. I'd pitch; I would not catch. You should probably consider going back to fucking the bench. I don't see how this can work out between us."

You see, I may make a few social faux pas and from what I've heard, a few of these guys can be bad tempered and might understand a thing or two I said.

And if by chance he won't take no for an answer, I'm having the burritos for dinner. After all, if it happens, I'm going to make it unpleasant for the both of us. If you want your pinga to wear a "poop soup suit," just give it a try. And I'm doubling up on the refried beans...you bastages.

Most of the time, I don't think I have an ego at all. But there are times, for a few freak seconds, where I'm convinced the sun rises just to impress me.

And it's not like I'm marching around saying, "I'm the greatest, blah, blah, blah me."

It's just that, when things happen, I think I'm saying for just a few seconds, that it's being done just for me.

An example? Ok. It is looking pretty good that pot is going to be legal in a few years... YAY!

Yes, it's beginning to look like our government has finally put a rope around its own waist and started yanking its head from its own ass.

There's a lot of good things going to be happening when it's legal.

For starters, my McDonalds stock will rise. I'm going to make millions from all the beginner smokers that will go pig out on Big Macs and fries. And I'm gonna start a McDonalds delivery service. That spells even more cash.

And a lot more stoner movies are gonna come out. These movies are designed to be "watched while actually stoned" movies.

Not to mention, it's gonna eliminate most depression. Sorry, but nothing is 100%. Example: You just smoked the last of your weed. Now you're high but a little depressed that you're out of weed. It happens.

Yeah, it's gonna be a good time to be a stoner. Now, my piece of weirdness was when I thought about if my mom was smoking weed. I'd think weed was so uncool then, that I wouldn't smoke it anymore.

So, for a few seconds I thought: they're legalizing weed so my mom can smoke it and that would bug me enough that I'd just quit.

Of course, I thought that while I was smoking weed.

———

I think the stupidest question I've ever been asked during an interview was last week for some mid-west magazine: Gophers and Gardens, I think.

It's the end of the interview and this dude says, "So, do you think any of the women you've slept with on the road only slept with you because you are famous?"

So, I'm like, "Really dude? You want to end a pretty good interview with a turd question like that? What 'interview' school did you graduate from that told you that's a good question to end an interview on? And you only got this interview because I promised your wife, while I was having sex with her…you shit, you… What was the question again? Oh yeah…, probably most of them."

So he's staring at me, and says, "WHAT!"

I repeated, "Probably most of them."

So his follow-up stupid question is, "Well, how did that make you feel?"

And I'm like, "Wow, ok… I couldn't care less. Beautiful women took me home and let me do anything I wanted with them, then let me leave. You can't go too much lower than a 'moral degenerate.' And you can only do that for so long.

I knew someday I would abandon that kind of life. It's tiresome being a pig and a whore.

I'm a lot more stable now. And I'm sorry if I insulted you before. And no, I didn't sleep with your wife. I don't fuck ugly women… Now what are you getting so upset about?"

Some people are so sensitive.

No matter how domesticated we become, nature is always around us. One day, I sat up in bed, and said, "My furniture used to be a tree. My clothes came from plants, like cotton. And my "pet rock" was, at one time, a wild rock."

Who I said all this too is still a mystery.

I'd like to meet the person responsible for the pet rock.

Somebody took a little box, put some grass or hay in it, and put a rock on top. That is your $5 "pet." And sold millions of them before somebody else said, "Why the hell would I want a rock for a pet?"

And the "pet rock" empire crashed with consumers crying about "buyer's remorse." We were never gonna buy anything so stupid again…

You know… until the mood rings came around again. Cocaine and disco made those crappy things popular again for 6 months.

Then we smartened up again for a bit…until Nancy Reagan's "Just Say No" T-shirts were everywhere. Everybody wore one. You almost had to just so you wouldn't be marked as a degenerate.

So I came out with my own "statement" T-shirt that read: "Just Say No to Saying No." And my label's name was F.T.B. I won't say what it means but the middle word is "That." I can't say the rest because "Ron" might crawl out of his grave and fuck me up.

Could you imagine him standing in front of you, and you're so star struck that you don't notice him ripping your heart out? He's throwing your heart from his left hand, back to his right, and back to his left.

In a couple seconds, the whole hero worship thing goes right in the toilet, "Dude, I think I want my heart back...right now."

I would fire up Ron's skeletal ass if I didn't get my heart back. Can you believe the decomposing, maggot-filled balls on this guy?

I self-medicate. Does it show?

———

So where is "Survivor" being filmed this season? I'm sure somebody is still watching it. I just want to say a thing about it...

It has nothing to do with actual surviving. It's a popularity contest; whoever balances being a kiss ass and a back stabber the best, wins some coconuts in a wheelbarrow or something.

What if they run out of islands? They might have to do a "Survivor Colorado." Two teams of 10 have to survive a month at an Aspen strip mall, and all its coffee shops.

Announcer: "Billy cannot be voted off this strip mall if he finishes this Blueberry Bull Latte. Let's go down to the inventor of this special drink...Derek. Derek, you invented the

Blueberry Bull Latte. Can you tell us how you made it?"

Derek: "Well sure. We take a cup of coffee and squeeze 10 blueberries in your hand; the juice then goes in the cup and we add some bull milk."

Announcer: "Ahhh, you can't milk a bull."

Derek: "Aahh, yes you can. And they really seem to enjoy it. You want a friend for life, go milk a bull. And since I bet $100 against that kid's team, I put in twice the milk and coated the entire cup with milk. When he's halfway done with it, I'm going to tell him what I did. If he throws up, he's off the strip mall."

Announcer: "You would really do that?"

Derek: "Oh yeah, with a big smile on my face. I'd be like, 'Dude, the secret ingredient is semen...animal semen.' Harold and Kumar, folks." Yeah, baby.

So my idea to make this a pay-per-view goldmine is get a real island, with quicksand and volcanoes; thousands of motion detector cameras and a ship load of death row inmates that will do anything to win this contest...and parole.

Oh, baby... Just think of all the carnage....

100 of the most disturbed men living in the deepest, darkest prisons we can dig up. All standing on a beach with no idea why they're there. You can't start telling them beforehand because they'd start building alliances with each other, and all that crap.

No. We just get them all on an island and then say over the loudspeaker, "Whoever survives the rough terrain for a month, gets paroled. Now divide into 2 teams and pick a captain." At this point, you don't feel obliged to say what game you're playing or if more than one can win. Let them figure it out.

You also don't have to have everyone speak the same language. That's another detail you let them worry about.

First guy that stands up and says he's a captain will find his hair parted with a coconut and a barrage of "Fuck you's."

Then you'll see just how much entertainment you can get for $39.95.

If you didn't take a pee during the last Pizza Hut commercial, you might just miss it. It could be like an old Tyson fight—90 seconds and done. Tyson pissed off a lot of my friends doing that.

Good meaning dummies that got up for a drink at the opening bell and come back 2 minutes later as Tyson was getting back into the limo.

That was the problem with having Tyson fight parties. There was always someone that showed up and, just as the fight started, there was a life or death crisis needing to be dealt with at that exact moment. And I'd say, "Wait till after the first round." But no. They knew best.

They leave. Fight starts. Fight ends. We're high-fiving each other and there's Johnny Derelict, "What happened?"

"Tyson jacked his shit up."

Now he's in a bad mood. Johnny didn't pay his $5 for the fight and now he's personally gonna drink all the beer he did not bring.

"Hey asshole, guess who's getting his wallet lifted as soon as he passes out?"

And if he had enough to tip us, which he did (back then), we had Chinese food delivered to a pizza parlor. Those guys put the Chinese food on a pizza and delivered it to a Spanish restaurant that folded the Chinese food covered pizza in half, deep fried it, and then delivered it to us.

It tasted like shit, but we were so hammered we ate it.

I'm thinking about learning Spanish. From the word on the street, by the time they start throwing dirt on my box, everyone here will be speaking it. I already know 2 words. "No" means no and "Chupacabra" means ex-wife. If you like irony, my ex-wife's maiden name was Chupacabra.

Who knew?

She also demanded I give her a nickname. I did better than that. I gave her 2 nicknames.

When life was smooth and everything was just peachy, I called her "Ruby." And when things were bad, she was the "Crazy Beaver." 'Crazy' cause DUH, she was my wife. Do you think I'd marry a normal female? And 'Beaver' cause of her overbite. When we get fighting and your overbite seems to grow.

A beaver was always what I thought her spiritual animal was. And when I see things in a largely childish way, I see her spiritual beaver say, "I'll be back in 5 minutes." And it starts gnawing on some spiritual pine tree. You know, real fast.

Know what I am? I am the world's slowest convert, from cheesesteak lover to vegetarian.

I hate the thought of animals being killed and ending up next to a large serving of garlic potatoes and apple sauce. But I do not live a meatless lifestyle. I've had neighbors tell that by the 4th meatless meal, in the middle of the night, when I was chasing squirrels with a butter knife in the snow.

Do you know what kind of meat question I'd love to ask one day? It's kind of a cannibalistic question, but...here goes: Does a vegetarian taste different than one of us meat eaters? I mean, how cool and ironic would it be if vegetarians tasted better, so we meat eaters would devour them?

If you're on the fence about coming back to the meaty side, now would be good timing.

———

Know what I'm in the mood to do now? I want to scare the shit out of young people. Not for long, maybe just a month or two.

Let's look at what's known as "Age Projection." It's not really called that, but it sounded official, didn't it? You gotta know how to improve bullshit. How about that? Did that sound more official? Yeah, that was more of the same.

So what happens when we hit the age of "30?"

Weight: It is impossible to lose a pound. You can suck down a billion salads, from Christmas to Easter, and you might lose 2-3 pounds, tops. And that's if you started bike riding again.

You sit there and stare at a candy bar for an hour before you decide if you'll eat it or not. Then you realize it takes 29,000 sit-ups to fix the damage caused by that dear, sweet piece of chocolate. (The friend that has now become an enemy even more frightening than those prison dudes on "Survivor.") And you'll finally say, "Fuuuuuuuuck that!"

My six pack turned into a keg before I knew it. I had to jog to the moon...and back...twice...before I could look down and see my...

Well, you know where this is going... And I'll tell you later on what goes wrong with that. And believe me, it gets scary even before that.

Let's discuss hair for a while.

Up until 30, you're pretty familiar with where all your hair has grown. And if you're not losing it, you're probably pretty happy where it is. But the day will come when you look up your nose and, instead of a little patch of peach fuzz, you'll have the "black forest" taking root up there. You will buy a good pair of tweezers...and you will pluck every hair...and you will cry... Why? Because it will hurt like a bitch.

And, as fun as the weekly harvest of nose hair is, let's take a look at those ears... Not just one...but both of them. Everywhere, there's hair. In it, on it, on top of it. And if you don't weed whack them, it looks like you're wearing earmuffs in July. Not the best look.

You learn that an hour a week will be donated to thinning out unwanted facial hair.

Then a few years after that, a big thing just bowls you over. You'll be looking in the mirror, just a-pluckin away, and you'll see an indentation on your face. Your first reaction will be, "Did someone slice my face with a knife while I was asleep? But it's not bleeding... Holy Shit, it's a fucking wrinkle!"

And for the next 3 weeks, you start shopping for coffins while having anxiety attacks.

Then you know you probably only have another good 30 years to go...I mean, another good 10 years with the following 20 years getting more painful by the minute.

Here's a couple of phrases you may want to bone up on while you're still young:

"Ow, my back is killing me."

"Ow, my shoulder is killing me."

"Who ate my last Viagra, dammit!?"

———

I got a chance to play God once...and I loved it. I manufactured someone's destiny. And before you start squealing like a stuck pig about how I shouldn't do stuff like that, I'll just say that the manufacturing had nothing to do with basements or chains.

So shut up and let me drive!

My buddy throws the best Super Bowl parties. The best food possible, and endless beer supplied. Not much not to like...except for Carl.

Carl likes to talk throughout the game...but not about the game. His focus (and mouth) are all about what's going on at his workplace. And when Carl talks, he usually has food in his mouth; or, at least that's where it starts.

Carl will fart in mid-sentence. And if someone stands up, Carl will ask that person for a beer whether he needs one or not.

So, I'm looking at Carl, and in my head I see giant neon letters in blue and green blazing and blinking on his giant, stupid forehead. These letters read: "VICTIM." Well, now it has to happen.

So I thought about it…

What does Carl like to do? Drink and fart; it's like he's a freakin 3 year old.

Soo…aha! A J.D. Express—2 parts Jack Daniels, 1 part powdered horse laxative. Just like Eric Roberts in "The Pope of Greenwich Village." But this is Carl the D-bag at my football party, of course.

Well, look what I have in my glove compartment. A bottle of Jack and powdered horse laxative. This must be my lucky night.

So I'm in the kitchen making the drink, and I call Carl in. I give him some bullshit story like, "I value our friendship, Carl, and I learned a lot about football from you. I appreciate my friends and I like to show them that with a private toast. Here's to our friendship, Carl."

And we drink. When he's done, I tell him to send Phil in.

Phil comes in, we do a shot, and I tell him, "Carl's gonna shit his pants in 5 minutes. Move away from him and send in Bob."

So everyone but Carl knows what's about to happen, and everyone has half an eyeball focused on Carl. He did not disappoint. After a Wendy's burger commercial, Carl says, "Here's what I think of your 'Baconator.' " Up goes the right leg and out flies 10 pounds of poop gravy.

Now, I like to pride myself for being able to think 5 minutes into the future, but this time I was tied up with abstract humiliation for one of God's lesser creatures and totally forgot about what the result of this prank would be. But, as luck would have it, he filthied up the one recliner that was going in the trash this week. (Whew!)

Carl couldn't get up. He had to sit in it, roll around in it and cry, like the big bitch he was.

After the rest of us stopped laughing, we each grabbed a corner of the recliner and carried it, and Carl, to the curb.

We threw him a towel, and said, "Good Luck, asshole."

That was the last we saw of Carl.

I looked out the window 20 minutes later and a couple of guys were putting the recliner in the back of their pick-up. It was dark, so they'll probably get a good look at it tomorrow.

I know I'd be mad at myself for grabbing a heavy chair like that only to find it has a 2 foot long "poop soup" stain on it. And it was probably still embedding itself ever deeper into the cushions.

Yup, that was me, playing God.

God (1) – Carl and the trash crap dudes (0).

When I was a kid, I loved scary movies. I wouldn't sleep for 3 days after, but they were great.

My mom taught me what to do if I was too scared to sleep. She said, "Remember, it's only a movie. They're actors, and the director is sitting right there in a chair to tell them what to do."

Imagine Boris Karloff as Frankenstein's Monster. He growls at the girl and it's a "bad growl," so the director leaps up, and says, "Cut...! Cut! Boris, what the hell kind of growl was that? What's the problem? Too much caviar in your dressing room? I can have that taken away.

"Look, you're trying to scare her. When you scare her, then you're also scaring the shit out of all the freaks that paid a nickel to be scared. Look at your script! It says right there, 'Monster: Big growl, big growl, little growl, big growl.'

"You did 'big growl, little growl, little growl,' and your last growl sounded like you burped at the end. Now, like it's written, let's go."

My mom could fix anything, even a scaredy cat.

And just for the record, Boris Karloff is one of my favorite actors and human beings.

––––––––

Know what makes me paranoid? No. Besides other people. It's being on a diet. My sensitivity goes through the freaking roof. I feel like everybody is looking and talking about me.

I was at the mall last week and there was this lady looking at me but talking out of the side of her mouth to her husband. And I heard her, even though there was noise everywhere. She said to her husband, "Why is that man on the bench crying?"

Cause I'm hungry, dammit! I love food and it makes me happy. I don't like walking out of a pizza parlor with only a salad in my gut. And, besides, it's an insult to the owner.

Oh yeah, I can justify anything thrown at me.

Except…commercials.

I think there's a camera in my TV and they are watching me. And they know when I'm dieting. Once they're sure, the roll the food commercials begin. "Folks, it's back! The tasty McRib sandwich. But only for a limited time."

I'm whipping through my date book, yelling at my TV, "That was only 11 months! You're only supposed to come here in April and it's only March…oh crap, it is April."

Maybe I'll freeze a dozen, so when I fall off the food wagon with a case of cold ones in my gut, I'll have something to beg forgiveness for that Sunday.

Can I get an Amen?

———

The gold medal for most deceiving TV munchies award goes to (drum roll): "Itty Bitty Petey Pete's Pizza" in California.

I'm sitting in the back room of some club out there, waiting to go on. I'm as high as the Redwoods, and I'm starving.

And there it was…the commercial of my dreams appeared. Itty Bitty Petey Pete's Pizza was advertising the "surf-and-turf" pizza. Huge chunks of sweet, succulent lobster, caught off the coast of Maine.

That is what they said.

And strips of filet mignon that will melt in your mouth.

They said that, too.

2 pizzas for only $9.99.

I was in love. I wanted a copy of the commercial, itself. It was the most beautiful pizza I ever saw in my life. It was like porn for the stomach. And yes, I was dieting then, too. I talked about it to my audience. I talked about it to the car driver after the show. And I talked about it to the waitress at Itty Bitty Petey Pete's restaurant.

"2 Surf-and-Turfs and a pitcher of beer."

I wanted that pizza.

What I got was pizza with beef jerky and tuna…it may have been cat tuna, it was so bad.

Isn't there some type of lawyer I can talk to about being disappointed like that? I mean, it's not as stupid as pouring hot coffee on yourself, but it still hurts. I just want to sue, at least a little bit. I just want enough to make that pizza a reality.

Alone. Silence. Grease rolling down my arms. Garlic frolicking on my tongue. And heaven…lobster, filet mignon being loved and sucked in so fast, I may actually lose a finger.

That would be the greatest 5 minutes of my life…

I love food. Oh my, when did I start crying?

Does the phrase "Have you ever been bitch-slapped?" sound like a threat to you? Me neither. Apparently, though, some police can actually manipulate that simple phrase to mean something else.

I know that for a fact. I may have said it on the side of the road one night to Officer Dempsey. We were discussing the pros and cons of coming to a complete stop at a stop sign.

My pros were, it saves me time and wear and tear on my breaks. His cons were, it's against the law and he saw me do it.

Now what the hell kind of debate is that?

Around about this time, I asked, "Have you ever been bitch-slapped?"

The next thing I remember is waking up in his back seat, handcuffed, and leaving a Dunkin Donuts on the way to the Police Station.

I like when someone says something stupid during a very sad time in order to break a heavy mood.

I was watching the Kurt Cobain suicide press conference years ago when the coroner walked up to the microphone, and said, "Mr. Cobain is no longer with us. And here is the instrument of his death that sprinkled his brain matter three counties over."

A reporter stands up. "So Mr. Cobain is dead?"

Your one time to ask a question and that's it, huh? I don't know what idiot said it, but there is such a thing as a stupid question.

And especially don't ask dumb questions in times of emergency. Like when the police are on strike because there's no money for raises, or the government shuts down because someone lost their anal beads. After all, there's really only one important question to be asked during such a crisis: Can we smoke pot yet?

Have you ever thought how you'd feel if your life was "The Truman Show?" Everyone you know is an actor, even Mom. Your whole existence is guided by a script written by some knucklehead that just pushes you in every direction to see how you'll react.

What if you don't even have a mom? What if your mom is a petri dish and your dad is a regular at the local sperm bank because he needs beer money on Friday nights?

Then you were implanted into a sheep's uterus until you were birthed in some lab at college. You were the original "Sheep Baby." Then, they circled a show around you.

The world sits and watches you think your daily life is real. I'd have to punch somebody in the throat.

But just in case it's true, if my scriptwriter happens to be reading this, try to be a little more discreet with the nose picking and masturbation. Would you, please?

Know what I really like to do? Fight. Just a good ole violent street fight. Someday I'm gonna win one. No, I'm kiddin…I always win. If you want to be brave enough to call me an asshole but not smart enough to carry a gun, well…that's your own damn fault.

The last time it came to that, this nitwit in a bathroom was in an "asking stupid questions" mood.

I was working on an engine block and I had to pee. So I walked into the men's room, washed my hands, peed, and then washed my hands again.

This guy was just kind of sitting around in there. I don't know why, but he asks me why I washed my hands before peeing.

I'm like, what? Why does this moron care? So I said, "Because your wife hates the taste of motor oil."

The guy had the nerve to take a swing at me. What's the matter with people today, anyway?

I would never go on a blind date that was set up by one of my friends. My friends are twisted. My friends would set me up with a shaved bear just to see my reaction.

I would have to add a few provisions to that blind date contract I would insist we have.

First provision: Must be a female and human. You would be surprised by what my friends will do for a laugh.

Second provision: Must be in the ballpark of what most men would agree looks like a woman. Hell, even in the same township would suffice. And if not, I get to punch the setter-upper in the mouth. That is provision 2A.

If she's a psycho but cute, I can deal with her senseless babbling. I'll just go a little deeper in my well of untried, wacky, crazy sex shit.

Lady, you are gonna pay for raping my ear.

And if you think that's cool, let the games begin.

If I get set up with someone that isn't technically a person anymore, I will climb out the bathroom window at the restaurant. I keep myself in good shape for just such a reason.

And every year, it gets harder. Either I'm getting bigger or the windows are getting smaller. I vote windows.

I think they should make mirrors cheaper. Obviously, some people don't have them. I mean, how can you leave the house in the morning looking like some do if you own a mirror?

I'm not talking about seeing two different shoes or socks, or the 55 year old man with the Led Zepplin T-shirt. I'm not even talking about the 500 pound woman wearing spandex. No, not these folks. If you think it looks great, then go for it. You folks keep the rest of us entertained.

What I mean is like, one collar up and one collar down; or your hair's going a thousand different directions.

Last week…man, this still grosses me out.

I was at a meeting. My agent introduced me to some executive from some cruise line and...oh, man...this guy has a huge zit on the end of his nose. And as he's talking to me, I'm watching this pocket of jello dance all over the tip of his nose. One side and then the other. I couldn't look this dude in the eye, I was so transfixed. It shook while he talked.

It was huge. It even took on some of the facial characteristics of its host...including, having a zit on the end of its own zit nose.

How can you leave the house with a virtual Siamese twin of pus hanging off your nose if you own a mirror?

It boggles the mind.

I wanted to buy it a hat and give it a name...Phil.

I purposely sat on my hands. My brain started talking to me. It said, "DO IT."

I could see listening to that order being unpleasant for both of us. Especially if I shot my eye out. I'd left my face shield at home.

Yeah, it really grossed me out. I still can't eat cream cheese.

Reality TV really pushes the limits, doesn't it? Unless you're willing to eat ground up goat testicles or fart the alphabet, you're just a dried-up, bitter old hack...yeah, like me. They ought to start to teach people something, or produce something that has a moral to it.

Here's one off the top of my head. God, I hate that fucking expression.

Oh yeah...the show... Have a show about how to lie to get out of work. And to save time and money with auditions...

I volunteer to do the show!

(Phone in hand) Cough, hack...cough..."Hello...Mr. Comedy Club Guy...cough...this is Bu...Bu...Buffalo Morgan. I don't think I can...cough...do the show tonight. I think one of your slutty waitresses got me sick last night."

Manager: "But Buff baby, sweetheart, we have that huge private party of lawyers."

Me: "Why those dirty rotten bastards! I'll be right there. I mean...cough, cough. I don't think I can make it...cough, cough. Why don't you put that waiter on who stirs the drinks with his...you know...oh yeah, cough."

Bosses hate the truth. Have you ever tried it with one? You learn to lie really fast.

Next Example:

Me: "Hey boss, how's it hanging? Hey, I'm gonna be a couple hours late today. The wife is all over me right now and I have to get it while I can. What do you mean "no"? Ok. Cough cough. I have strep throat. I'll see you tomorrow. (Click) You old bastard...

Oh shit, I thought I hung up.

———

You know who else hates lying? Any woman I date. They think they hate lying, but they don't. Ever see how sad a woman gets when you tell them the truth about something they don't want to know about?

Tell them the truth and they start crying...and cursing...and threatening to put radiator fluid in your next drink.

Knowing all this, why go with the truth? And they'll lie first, anyway.

Guys, know how we like to disappear for, I don't know, like a week, or even a couple days without even a phone call to let anyone know where we are? And the moment you get home, the wife is all over you with, "Where have you been? Why didn't you call? Why was your bookie knocking on our door with a bat?"

She sounds like she's in one of her "actual and precise" moods. But she's not.

I always start off honest, but then when she lies to me, I just lie right back to her. This is how honest I get.

"Ok, honey, now do you want the story where we both can feel great about the love we feel for each other, or do you want the truth that reeks of shame and debauchery?" Sounds like a common sense question, right? Know what she chooses? Right, the truth.

So…that's a lie, and I lie right on back to her. I just wish I could stop saying, "Once upon a time…" before I begin this tapestry of bullshit. Kind of a dead giveaway that a lie is on its way. I'll get better, though.

Little tip for the guys out there. Take a sip of radiator fluid, just to get a quick idea of what it tastes like. It's a good thing to know about. If your macaroni and cheese has a funny little taste to it, believe me, she's still pissed.

Actually, women enjoy it when you lie to them. They love to hear a man's creativeness. They do. Give them a fantastic tale then, near the end, pull the story to the right and watch her eyes just light up.

Up until the moment you say, "And they all lived happily ever after," she is on the hook. Take that however you want to.

If you ever get a chance to screw over a pingahead, do it. Do it…and love it.

I was getting my lottery tickets a couple nights ago; I have my numbers already on the sheets, so I'm in and out of line in ten seconds or less: THE WAY IT'S SUPPOSED TO BE DONE! (Hint, fucking hint.)

I got there just 3 minutes before the lottery went off, and this big dude comes racing through the door, bangs my shoulder, and says, "Hurry up, dude."

So I slowly turned to face him, and said, "I'll be done in a minute." Then I turned back to the guy selling the tickets, "So explain this lottery thing to me, buddy."

"DUDE!"

Slowly I turned again and, after a nice long stare, I said, "Yes?"

And this idiot is in such a craze, he begins spitting his words at me. I thought the roof had sprung a leak. "Dude, the lottery goes off in two and a half minutes and I don't have my tickets yet."

I smiled, "Really? I didn't know that…huh."

Then I faced the cashier again, "So explain what those button-like buttons do."

He knew I was playing with this guy, so he said, "Come on, Buff."

I knew he didn't want me rolling around the aisle with this big dummy so I let it go. I hand him my cash and he hands me my tickets. As I'm taking my tickets from his hand, I say, "Hey, I just saw a kid drinking a soda over there."

As these 2 guys are looking around, I quickly unplug then re-plug in the lottery machine. They take 5 minutes to reboot. Guess who's not getting his freakin' tickets?

By the time they figured out what had happened me, and my Porsche-encrusted ass, are skidding sideways out of the parking lot with the appropriate finger extended through the moon roof.

Now there are a lot of morals to be learned from that story, but I think the most important one is: "Do not touch me unless you're a hot chick."

You guys know what a crack head is, right? How about a gloryhole? Wow, you guys are pretty worldly. Ok, we'll stick to gloryhole life for the moment. And you never know...? Gush, gush.

Come to think of it, there may just be a connection. I mean, you don't know who's on the other side of that wall. There may be a picture of Marilyn Monroe on the wall, but I can assure you that's not her working your junk over for 5 bucks.

I was invited to one, so I went. I needed some new material. This sounded too freakin funny. And when I got there, it was just how I thought it'd be.

And I laughed my ass off.

3a.m. in a small office. Guys, some older men, maybe 30 of them, were waiting for a hole to open up where some other guys are having someone in another room give them oral sex.

See...there's this hole. You stick $5 in, and then your pinga goes in. I mean...like for 10 minutes, I couldn't stop laughing.

Then I got creeped out...big time. I think I might have seen too many episodes of "The Walking Dead" for this particular event.

Really, this is what members of our species do. I'm amazed another mammal hasn't tried to take over. I don't know, maybe polar bears. Actually, it's not a bad idea. But not polar bears. We need something that would be easy to take out of power once we cleanse ourselves of the shit that we've become.

How about cats? Cats look like they're studying how to take over the planet anyway.

The shift of supremacy is now set upon the narrow shoulders of the common house cat. "You want the power? Take the fuckin power. But know, we'll be back."

As soon as we get that second big bang, which will be more of a pop as your head comes flying out of your rectal cavity.

Then we will move back up to the top of the food chain. So sometime during that first week of being a second class citizen to a freakin cat in power, go to your local dollar store and pick up a spray bottle.

That is the weapon that will guarantee you will have your throne back.

And it's not just the gloryholes that make me think a large portion of the male population should be exterminated. It's the other little thing, too, that really gets under my freakin skin. Any guesses what?

(Guy in the audience): "Bad oral sex."

"Bad oral sex? No such thing. Anybody else?"

(Lady in the audience): "People that don't use their turn signals."

"You are absolutely correct, madam."

———

You've seen my show before. I'm honored you came back, and a bit surprised." Wait, did I just say that out loud?

"I've been working here too long at the Fabulous…Hellhole Comedy Club in beautiful Las Vegas." Yeah, 5 bucks. The owner gives me 5 bucks every time I mention the club. I do it because I'm a whore. Every extra 5 is another hit of crack…uh, I mean, gets me closer to sending my…uh, kid to college? Yeah, that's it.

"The only crack I'd like to smoke is Jessica Alba's. Oh shit, that's another thing I shouldn't have said out loud. Wouldn't that be funny if Jessica Alba was in the audience tonight? And she loves my act and takes me home for a couple dozen shots of tequila? Oh my god, I just smiled way too wide for that fantasy."

Wait a minute. A small lifetime ago I was talking about cats being at the top of the food chain.

Right... We humans gave them the power. Cats can now think and talk. And they're very condescending, but that hasn't really changed.

I'd probably have to drive my cat everywhere. And since I'm always pissed off when I drive, that's probably where I'd snap.

She'd be sitting in the back seat like Miss Daisy and just bitching about whatever cats bitch about. "I hate that new flavor of Meow Mix. Buy that again and I'll make you eat it. Did you see that mouse in the living room? Call an exterminator when we get home. I'm a cat, I'm number one. You're a person, you're number two."

And I'd be clenching the steering wheel in a death grip, head between my shoulders, and my right eye uncontrollably twitching.

Then, I have a white out. Next thing I know, we're not even in the car anymore. I'm chasing her across somebody's farm with a spray bottle.

And that's why I think cats would be better than polar bears to run the planet. Spray bottles wouldn't work on polar bears. He'd look down at you, and say, "What, are you freakin kidding me?"

———

Getting back to crackheads. If someone calls you, say, crackhead Steve, 9 times out of 10 you're probably a crackhead. Yes, they're on to you.

If people call you crackhead Steve and your name is Steve and you smoke crack, then that's your name. We'll just assume you have a head…big and bloated as it is.

The first time I met a crackhead was at a playground. This skanky ho…or ugly bitch, whatever you want to call her, told me she'd lick any body part of mine for ten minutes for ten bucks.

I said, "Make it 5 bucks." I guess times were tough. 5 bucks, baby!

That is where I became a man, at 10 years old. And she was terrible at it. This was my first sexual experience and I knew even back then it was bad.

I don't know what felt better. The fact that someone other than myself touched me, or that I saved 5 bucks? I tried to slip her an I.O.U., but she kind of went ballistic.

"Ok, here's some cash." Then I made a rookie mistake. All I had was twenties, so I made her swear she'd bring me back the change. 2 days later...no change.

I did see her a week later. She told me how she got robbed on the way to the store. Then she said she'd do that neat little trick again for another 5. When she was done, I handed her a napkin to wipe her chin.

And she said, "That's ok. I'm good." Then she ran out the door.

So every Friday after school, I had a steady date. Sometimes, I'd tell my friends what was going on. I charged them each 2 bucks to stand behind a bush and watch.

I was making some real money and she was getting better. Life was good. I thought it was a great business until my little princess got busted. Then it dawned on me, like, ohhh...that's what was going on.

What do you want? I was ten. There probably a lot of them around, but I'm oblivious to it until something really obvious happens. Like when I was a sheet metal mechanic....

I walked into the bathroom as Charlie was walking out. When he said "hey," I swear I saw a tiny bit of smoke follow his greeting, and the bathroom stunk…Damn!

So I asked a couple of my coworkers and they said he was a crackhead. I didn't believe it, so I decided to test Charlie. I left a fingernail-sized piece of drywall on top of the sink in the bathroom. Then I waited for Charlie to go in and out. When he left, I went in and, guess what? The rock was gone and it smelled like burnt drywall in there. So, to wrap this whole Crackhead/Gloryhole thing up nicely, if I have to chuppa pinga to get high, I don't want to get high.

I think I'll do puzzles or fly a kite.

That'd be funny, though, if a gloryhole needed to hire more employees. They'd put a sign outside that read: "Help Wanted: Apply Behind Wall."

And I wonder how long orientation would be? "Ok boys, you all did great on the true and false questions. Now for a little on-the-job training.

Phil, there's your first customer. Go wrap your pretty little lips around that thing. They'll do the rest. It's like a big purple apple, isn't it, Phil? AAANNNDDD finish. Ok class, is there anything you saw Phil do that looked right or wrong, that you have questions about? You, in the third row."

"It looked like a couple of times, he bit him."

"Yes, very good. Do not bite. Most do not enjoy it. Anybody else? Yes, you."

"He didn't get paid up-front, or at all."

"Excellent, you're not doing this for the fun of it. You're doing it to make money to get high. Number one rule."

Do I want to get high this bad?

No F.W.

I've just been handed a note. The kitchen says they're out of chicken soup and there's only New England clam chowder left.

Happy Guzzling. Gush, gush.

Women, yum yum. But man, do we have to work for it. And I don't mean little things like calling you from the pharmacy for your tampon size, or do you want wings or no wings? Or going to the pharmacy to pick up your prescription only to find an old, deaf and blind woman running the counter. (I don't even think she knew she was working there.)

After about 10 minutes, I'm starting to get annoyed. "It says 50 tablets of penicillin, what do you get?"

"The word penicillin is spelt wrong. Do you want me to give you the wrong medicine? Or are you one of those "penicillin junkies?"

Now I'm pissed. "PENICILLIN. GIVE ME MY PENICILLIN."

That turned a lot of heads.

And you know they were all thinking the same thing. "That dirty bastard has V.D."

Well, I don't. It was for my girlfriend at the time. She was having one of those crotch-bread things.

"A yeast infection?"

Yes, that's it...a yeast infection. Thank you very much. I knew it had something to do with bread. I can never remember that disease, because the only time I hear about it is when someone is telling me she has it.

I pick up accents as soon as I hear them. Sometimes I scare myself, it's so quick. I did a show in Georgia last summer and, when it was over, I went to the bar...duh, I know...and this good ole boy wanted to have a drink with me.

So he starts talking, "Man, dude, that was funny shit man; I mean I peed my denims, man. Like shit, man, you know what I mean? I mean, were you really smoking dope up there?"

So I said, "No man, you crazy. The great state of Georgia would just bury my ass, I tell you what. But the Thanksgiving bit where I snorted a line of salt...that wasn't salt." So he's waving his arms around like, I don't know...a maniac.

"Come on, man, let's go get a keg and some girls. I have a cabin far out in the woods."

Ok, so now I'm thinking: "escape."

———

I am not going out in the woods with Ricky Redneck and lethal doses of alcohol. Follow me on this. The beer shows up at the cabin—the girls don't—guess who has the pretty mouth then?

So my mind starts formulating a plan: go to the bathroom and climb out the window. Brilliant...how I love this fucking brain.

And you know something? That stupid plan worked. I jumped into my car, filled up at a gas station, where I also purchased a pound of beef jerky and a couple of guns…big ones. That dude looked like a .22 just wouldn't slow him down. And I ran my ass back to Jersey.

Once I got about 3 or 4 tolls into New Jersey, I was pretty sure I was home free. I also have to stop watching "Deliverance" before I go out on tour.

"But I don't want to squeal like a pig." Fuck that.

Let's face it, it's always better if your woman calls you immature than premature.

I can actually help you if you happen to be premature. That happens when your mate feels too good. You have to dull the ecstasy back a notch. I suggest wearing about 10 condoms at a time.

And if that don't work, take a marker and draw a 19th century handlebar moustache on her. Of course, this only works if she happens to be facing you. Remember, there's a lot of positions to try.

But we're supposed to be talking about immaturity.

I want to. I want to. I want to.

"No."

"Yes, my show. I talk about immaturity or I leave."

"Fine."

Folks, the other half of my Brain has arrived. Go on Holmes, take a bow. There you go, when Rolling Stone magazine does a story on me, I'm going to say that.

Rolling Stone: "So Buffalo, is there anything about you that nobody knows?"

Me: "Yes, I call the left side of my brain Holmes."

Rolling Stone: "And the right side you call...what?"

Me: "Why would I name the right side? Who took my plate of coke? I said a bottle of Italian wine! This is French. Know what? This interview is over." How's that for immature?

I'm a different type of immature. I like sitting cross-legged on the floor, and occasionally, I'll have Cocoa Puffs for dinner. I've had women tell me that is immature.

Know what I said? FINE. And you know what that means, right? Fine?

I know it's usually a woman thing, but I'm hijacking it. I hear guys say "fuck you" all day and it's tiresome. If I can spew just one less "fuck you" into our atmosphere, then it is worth it, ok? Fine.

And you saw how I said it, right? Kind of how I'd imagine Boris Karloff would say it. If you have your arms and legs crossed, standing in a doorway with your head tilted back to catch the warm summer moonlight in your brown smokey eyes. No matter how you say "fine," you're not going to come off good.

And I count how many times you make me say "fine" every day. And eventually I start deducting money from what I had planned to get you on your birthday. It could be a $1000 three-night stay at the nicest hotel in town, and you might whittle it down to a much lesser "nice."

And if you have it engraved, remember that she might use that lighter to burn down your home. If you would like to be identified by your dental records, write something like this...

"It was this or the Fontaine Bleu."

"You'll make a great smoker."

And if you want to be lit up right then and there, have it engraved with, "Fine." She's a woman, she knows what the word means. So you might want to wear about 3 cups and a pair of fire-retardant Levi's. Remember when I told you how upset your woman will get if you call her the C-word, using a finely crafted "woman's word" like "fine" against her? You're toast. The ass kicking you'll get from that will make the C-word beating look like a simple bitchslap.

I would say Chinese women are the worst drivers in the world.

Hey, who just called me a racist? I have 2 words for you. Let's see if you can guess what they are.

I'm not a racist. I dated a Chinese woman for 5 months, so I know what I'm talking about. In that 5 months, she hit 3 opossums, 1 raccoon, 2 pigeons, a robin, a deer, and a dolphin. She should hunt with a Chevy. Then there were the 2 trees, a pole, 4 signs, and a wide assortment of other cars. Most of those came from parking.

It's like whatever she's trying to avoid, she points the car towards it. Then she closes her eyes and prays.

And that's all been when I'm in the car. Who knows how much more destruction there is when I'm not in the car. She stopped telling me stories once I started putting her stories in my act. The last month we dated, she started telling me a story of a near-sighted rabbit, then, when she realized I might tell that story over the weekend, it changed to: "Then I hit...uh, I mean, the rabbit hit my car."

It got to the point where I started carrying a machete around on our dates. Just in case I have to chop off your dumbass head because you're hurting and you were too fucking stupid to stay in the goddamn woods.

The dolphin? Yeah, I know what I said. No, a jet ski. Here's the quickie version of it...

She's driving us on a jet ski in the blue water of the Bahamas. A string of dolphins are following one another and she wants to get a closer look.

So the dolphins go down...come up...go down...come up...they go down, and I'm thinking, "We are too close." Then I hear her say, "Oh, f...," and we went airborne off the poor bastard's head.

What started out as a beautiful day watching 12 majestic dolphins sailing through the gentle waves, turned into 11 dolphins frantically trying to escape us and the headless corpse of their buddy, lifelessly bobbing in a never-ending pool of its own blood. (Yeah, I brought the machete on vacations we had, too.)

Too dark? Know what's dark? The soul of my proctologist. This dude may look at you, but I think there's "nobody home;" you know, upstairs. When he gets done doing what he does, he always has a twisted smile on his face.

One time I asked him what he is thinking about as he was jamming his finger in my ass. Know what he said? "Car payment." Then, WHAMMO!

If he didn't look like a ghoul from a cheap 1930's horror flick, I'd hang out with him. It'd be hilarious getting this guy hammered and watch him trying to function. I'm such an ass.

I did that to one of my cousins one time. He touched alcohol once in college; he told me he wanted the whole "Buffalo Morgan experience." He came to a show, then we bar hopped 'til we hit a party. But in one of the bars, I asked him if he wanted to sing some karaoke. It wasn't a karaoke bar, but he didn't know that. Except for knowing that a bar like that would be where you sang, he didn't actually know what karaoke was. So he went to the juke box and picked out a song. I told him the microphone was broke, so just sing louder.

Then I stood up on my stool and got everybody to be quiet. Then I announced: "Good evening. My cousin always wanted to do karaoke. He's never seen it done or even knows what a karaoke machine is." The whole time I'm winking. "So give my cousin a warm round of applause." And out of this 100 person-filled bar, only 2 clapped.

So the song starts and he's standing on his stool, more yelling than singing to Bob Seger's "Night Moves."

I was pissing myself laughing. Everyone had their drinks in their hands and their mouths hanging open, but everybody was too stunned to drink. When he was done, there was no applause. Just a wall of voices I couldn't understand except for one couple that said, "What the fuck was that?"

It was about this time that management from the club suggested we leave...NOW.

But...getting back to my proctologist; he's good. Skinny fingers and he's quick. And it's always gimmicky to him. Some proctologists think it is one big joke. "Ok, here comes the airplane into the hangar."

My boy is quick; you don't know the old airplane is coming. Last time I was in his office, he asked me to pick up a pen behind me. I did and...WHAMMO! That'll straighten the curly hairs a bit. I'll bet nobody slouches in his family.

It's important to pick out the right doctor. And dentist, too. I searched years for a good dentist. And when I say, "good," I mean, "quiet." Why do some dentists insist on holding a conversation with you when your mouth is full of fingers, cotton, and numbness...oh, and that hose that sucks up your drool?

I always come off sounding like Fat Albert's buddy, Mushmouth. "Well bu, I bu think by the Eagles bu could bu make it to bu the Super Bowl...bu."

This one dentist gave me his life story in the first ten minutes of a cleaning. Then he asked me what I thought. And I always speak from the gut, a stupid habit I picked up somewhere.

What I should have said was, "Well, that's nice." Then shut up. What I did say was, "You sound like a real tool. Now shut the fuck up and clean my teeth...bu."

See, now that is not the proper way to speak to someone in the medical field, especially when they are working on you.

It's also not good to talk like that to someone handling your food. You don't want your egg drop soup to be gooier than before or your won ton soup to taste like urine.

It's always in the soup. They respect their entrees too much. There are some places where the people that prepare food are brain dead. Case in point...

A couple years ago I was in a restaurant. I ordered a cheeseburger and all the junk that comes with it. So out comes the burger, carried by my waitress, Ashley. So there were my fries, my beer, and my Texas bacon burger on a blood covered bun.

What the fuck are you people thinking?

There are pools of unquagulated blood on the bun, the burger, and the plate. Someone in your kitchen is having a serious problem right now. And I can't believe you're so deep in the fog, you'd put that plate down in front of me. I'd sue you, except I've got no use for a double-wide that's sitting on bricks about to be repossessed.

I ended up taking it back to the kitchen and pelting the cook in the back of the head with it. He turned around, really deliberate, like he had something to say. Once he saw the "I'm going to kill you" look on my face, he had nothing to say. Did you not think I'd notice blood stains over half the roll?

And if I'm going to start bitching about people who I think should be beaten, it's people that insist upon taking your parking space, even before you get into your car. When I notice I'm being used in this manner, I drag my ass.

Especially if I think you need to drop a few pounds. Get the hell up and walk!

I was gonna run for president one year but my opposition found the porno I had made like, 20 years before. I didn't really believe I'd win. I think it was more to build my credits to my intro.

How cool would that sound?

"And here he is (drum roll), actor, author, model, comedian, and former presidential candidate...Buffalo Morgan."

Sounds a little better than your average show pony, don't you think?

If I was president, I'd have to be single. Could you imagine the caliber of women I'd have dancing through the White House? I'd be signing some of the most important documents on the backs of some of the most beautiful girls in the world.

I wouldn't even know where to begin to run for president. What do I do? Like, run for mayor?

Actually, I've heard good things about being mayor. Like, you're driving around in parades with a pitcher of Pina Colada at your feet. And when you go to restaurants, you don't have to pay. You sing a couple napkins and they're happy as shit.

I can see that only workin once or twice in each restaurant. By the third time, the owner would probably like to have a talk with you. "Mayor Morgan? (See how good that sounds?) Enough with the autographs. Go into your wallet and find me some dead presidents."

And let's not forget the best part about being mayor. A couple times a year, the mayor is allowed to stuff his pockets with taxpayer money, then get a motel, a hooker, and a big bag of crack. Isn't that like, "The American Dream?" I'm pretty sure the rest is, like signatures and handshakes.

In 1940, the media had respect for celebrities and politicians. Now they hunt them for scandal. And people just lap it up. Back then, if you were single and kissed someone in public, you got a bad reputation.

That'd be funny if that kind of morality circles back in about 200 years and 2 people are having a discussion about People magazine's archives they found.

Bob: "Hey Bill. Ever heard of the Kardashians?"

Bill: "Yeah Bob. They were a family of piobenias that ate an Olympic swimmer."

Bob: "But what were they famous for?"

Bill: "Well, I think the fat one was in Playboy."

Bob: "And that's how they all got famous?"

Bill: "No, it looks like they had a TV show, and if I'm reading this story right, the daughters were in competition to see who banged the ugliest guy in California."

Bob: "And our ancestors used to watch this shit?"

Bill: "Yeah, for a while it was a highly rated show."

Bob: "Wow, that's really fucked up."

Bill: "You said it, brother."

Bob: "And look at all these actresses getting out of cars with no underwear on. What were they all? Cheap sluts?"

Bill: "Well, that goes without saying, Bob."

Bob: "And look at this story. Actor gets 6 months for marijuana possession."

Bill: "Well, that's amazing. Pot's been legal for 50 years. It's hard to believe the law makers were so stupid back then."

Bob: "Yes, they were stupid. They were very, very, very stupid. Practically brain dead."

You see what I'm doing right? If I can get an F.B.I. file on me, it goes right onto my intro.

"Here he is (drum roll...we have to keep drummers in business), actor, author, model, comedian, former presidential candidate, and now being investigated by the F.B.I., Buffalo Morgan." It all adds to the mystery.

———

It took me 48 years and a couple continents, but I did it. I found my dream house. It's in Scotland. It's close enough to Ireland; I'll just think of everyone being Irish.

Of course, you can't say that. That would really piss a Scot off.

"What the devil did you say, lady?"

"I said, Mr. Shalaly Breath, could you direct me to the nearest brothel? I want an authentic female leprechaun."

"Why you ignorant Yankee turnip, dis here be Scotland. That flucking isle of deprivation lies 200 kilometers over da horizon in the middle o' the pond."

"...What?"

That would be my usual first impression to my neighbor. It's a challenge. Let me see if I can get my neighbor to hate me in 2 sentences or less.

Then it's the typical growth of a Scottish friendship. You bump into each other at the same pub. You drink. You beat each other black and blue. And when you sober up, you're best friends.

Let's get back to my house, which is really a castle. And not a big "Addam's Family" house that looks a little like a castle. I mean a giant house that branched off to other buildings and is surrounded by a 30 foot high, 10 foot thick wall. There is fishing in the moat. How freaking cool is that? When you cross the drawbridge, there is a golf course half a mile away.

But it needs some work. You know, little things like bathrooms. I know some women are good sports but not enough to squat over a hole and "let it fly." However, that may be a good way to find a good woman.

"Now Lisa, are you sure you don't mind?"

"Are you kiddin? Tonight I might try and poop my longest poop, and I can't do that sitting down."

(The heartbeat races...) "I...I think I love you."

So I was thinking yesterday, the reason we eat and...you know...defecate, is because we move. We do things, and all those things we do require a lot of energy.

Now look at a tree. It does nothing but grow and make leaves. It uses no energy except for that. So the sun, some water, and the nutrients in that water is all a tree needs to grow.

And that thought came from a previous thought the day before. I was thinking then about when you die and go to heaven—you do not eat food as we know it. Otherwise, it'd constantly be raining turds. And except for one freakin seagull, I walk the Earth, turd free.

Which leads to this point. If we don't eat, then we probably don't drink. So if we don't drink, then we can't make bodily fluids. So sex is probably non-existent. And that sucks, because when is the last time you saw a picture of an ugly angel? They're all hot, am I right?

So it's like you have a whole heaven full of beautiful angels and you really can't do anything with them.

They're all like brothers and sisters. So we just walk around doing angel stuff, and that's it.

Sounds almost like a practical joke. "When does it end, Lord?"

In what plane of existence can I have it all? I don't think he likes me.

And that heavy thought comes to me from my courteous friends out in the fields, working hard to grow only the finest weed. Thank you, folks.

––––––

So, occasionally people ask me if I ever get mad. I guess my warm and humble demeanor really shines on stage. And if you're thinking about that, then I have just 2 words for you...and if you think you're so smart, then figure that out.

I get mad, but usually at myself. Like last weekend: I killed 6 hours watching TV and there was nothing on. 1195 channels...and there was nothing on. After spinning through a dozen times, I finally picked the best of the worst. Kind of the same way I vote. So I ended up watching an operation of some lady that got her face ripped off by a chimp. It was a lot less cool than it sounds.

And why would someone want to own a chimp? They're famous for three things: Ripping off people's faces, flinging warm handfuls of monkey poop at people, and the classic, dressing like a chauffeur while smoking a big cigar.

Even though number 3 is hilarious, I can see the novelty wearing off in a month or two. But the first 2 would probably make me paranoid after a while. Every night, I'd be barricading myself in my bedroom.

Eventually I start doing silly things, like testing my food for poison. During lunch, I take a couple kung fu lessons.

I know one day we'll have a sit down to talk out our problems.

Me: "Ok, monkey, I finished painting a white line down the center of the house. That is your side. If you come over to this side, I will kung fu your balls to Saturn…and, if by chance you have no balls, I'll blow your little monkey brains all over the carpet.

Oh, and by the way, the guy is coming over on Monday to Scotch-Gard the carpets, so find some place to go."

Monkey: "Ok, you can use it twice a day, but only when I'm out." (HEY, in my paranoid delusions, my monkeys talk. And use toilets!)

I do have a couple solutions to curb "monkey on people" violence, though.

One is to toilet train them. A lot of times when they show pictures of monkeys walking freely in people's houses, they are wearing diapers. Do you not think chimps get humiliated too? Be happy he doesn't take more than your face.

And if that turns out to be a bad idea, smoke some pot with the little shit maker. He may attack the Doritos stash, but violence is usually confined to humping your sofa...so you might want to Scotch-Gard the sofa, too.

But don't worry, monkeys are famous for having tiny pingas. A gorilla has a full 4 inches.

Did you know you can make a gorilla cry by laughing at his junk? Wait, maybe the gorilla rips your arms out of the sockets if you laugh at his junk. I forget which.

Hey, if somebody is going to the zoo anytime soon, could you do a little field research for me?

But the point I'm trying to make is that the medical field can give you a new face, arms and legs, and any new organ...except a brain, which is another God-like, practical joke. (Haha, something we actually need.)

Anyway, medical science can fix just about anything...except male pattern baldness. I know they have tricks.

Like taking hair from the back of your head and planting it in the front. And if you have curly hair, they take it from somewhere else. (I was thinking chest hair, but you can have them take it from wherever you want...sickos.)

Hold on! The problem solving side of my brain is kicking in...

Ok, if you have male pattern baldness and want to own a chimp, try to find a chimp with the same hair color. If you get a hair transplant, they can take the hair from the chimp. You'll look great and the monkey will look funnier...he's a monkey, fuck em. Flip the mirrors towards the walls and he'll never know. See? Problem solved.

———

I really hate moronic people. Once upon a time, I had a cubicle. That's right, I was white collar, no shit.

And this dingaling in the next box kept making drug jokes with people all around us. He came to one of my shows and got my whole deal.

One day in July, he walks over to my box, and says, "Hey man, it's snowing downstairs."

That's code for "my cocaine dealer is waiting for me in the lobby." Conveniently, he used to show up every payday. Sorry, but I had to explain that to the people who never had cocaine delivered to them at work...and I'm sorry I had to explain that.

So he's like, "Hey man, it's snowing downstairs."

And I'm like, "Hey man, shut the fuck up."

Another time, I'm coming out of the bathroom as he's going in, and he says, "Hey man, sniff sniff, how is it?"

This time I was ready for him. I said, "What, your mother? She's a fat, old slut. And I only bang her because she's slightly better than self-abuse."

Now, I may have overreacted just a bit, but he didn't talk to me the rest of the time I worked there. Can't argue with those results.

I also booby-trapped his life. He seemed like a rat, so after that day with the mother bit, I taped two $20 bags of coke to the underside of his desk. He'd never know they were there. So if I ever got called into the office on an anonymous tip that I had coke allegedly delivered to the business, guess who's gonna be drug tested with me?

Me: "But boss, I never even seen cocaine. But I've seen Dale taping something under his desk. And one time he said it was…what did he call it? Oh, yeah, cocaine."

And once they find it, we'll both be drug tested. I'll be clean.

That's a fact. But Dale won't.

When I got his coffee, they were out of sugar at 7-11 that day. So I spiced it up with cocaine. He's going to be blowing fire into that piss cup.

"Remember when you said this was the best cup of coffee you've ever had, Dale? Well, put it together…there you go…you figured it out."

He'll probably be denied unemployment, any employment, and welfare. I'll bet within a month, he'll be swallowing hotdogs to buy hamburgers. And let this be a message to the rest of you.

Aww, come on, you know I'm kidding. You folks look smart enough to leave me and my drug habit alone.

So how many of you are convinced I'm a drug addict? No, not coke. Just some tasty lawn clippings. Yum, yummy. I'm old. One more hit could blow my heart up like a balloon. Do you know how fucking stupid I'd feel overdosing at this age? I'd be found with rings around my nostrils, straw in one hand and the other hand down my underwear.

I can see that picture flying around YouTube. There's like 10 million comments on it: "What a shame. (snicker) What an asshole."

When I do something stupid that's going to get me killed, I want to go out respectably. Like on top of a beautiful woman, half my age.

Or if my death can help somebody. Like if a speeding Pepsi truck runs a red light and field goal kicks my ass through the Pearly Gates, my kids will own Pepsi.

I'll bet you're wondering why I started talking about death. Well, I went to my doctor last week and he said I probably have, at the most, another 50 years. So now I have a new goal. I want to live to be 100 so I can make my doctor look like an ass.

I can be as petty as the next bastard.

Every season has its piece of specialness to show that even though we're human, we're still dumb as animals. Not me, of course. But I'm sure we all know someone that isn't all there...and if you don't, your friends probably do. Yes, take that personally.

———

I think winter is the best. I like watching people that think the laws of ice do not apply to them.

They just go strutting across a parking lot...then, WHAM! On the ass, then on the head. Hey, we've all fallen on the ice. The trick is to not fall in front of people.

I'm a bit of a connoisseur about this. In theory, the bigger the person, the funnier the wipeout. Smaller people in the act of falling accept the fact that in a nanosecond, their ass is gonna hurt. Bigger people tend to wave their arms in circles hoping for something to grab onto. I've actually moved my arm out of the way when a behemoth next to me started to fall.

I know, not too heroic, but there was no way I was going down, too.

Our eyes met as she was falling. Her eyes said: "Help me kind sir, I'm falling."

My eyes replied: "Ffffuuuuuuuuuckkk that."

Yeah, I saw it in slow motion. Then my eyes said: "I have to look away because I'm about to start laughing."

Ten seconds later, when I could not control myself from laughing, I turned back around to help her. But by that time, she was already in her car, driving away, giving me the finger. She moved pretty quickly for a big girl. And I don't blame her for the finger. I think it's the fear in the eyes that was funny. Does that make me a bad person? And if someone slipping on the ice is funny, then a car doing 360's down a highway is downright hysterical.

A couple winter's ago, this Chevy was spinning past me on an icy highway; the driver was facing me for about 2 seconds. He had a death grip on the steering wheel and it looked like he was yelling, "Help me." Obviously I couldn't hear him, but that's what it looked like.

So I cracked a smile, and gestured, "What would you like me to do?"

On his next spin by, he gave me the finger, too. It must be the cold weather. But then again, he looked scared. Maybe fear triggers the "sacred bind." I don't think it's my laughter. Laughter is supposed to be contagious.

The last good laugh I got was watching this big dude waddling up and down the aisles of a drug store. The little voice in my head said, "$20 he's looking for Preparation H."

Sure enough, he grabbed the biggest tube he could find. I'll bet his toilet is a wreck. He probably has Roto Rooter on speed dial: "Yeah, it's bad. It was taco night at the bowling alley... Yeah, I'd bring a couple helpers... Yeah, the window's open and I have about a dozen candles lit."

———

Public bathrooms are another way to see how the other half lives. How can people miss so badly? Guys are bad, but women have told me they're worse. How? All your equipment is pointing down. Are you really that bad with directions? Do you use that much thrust?

I've had lots of different women over to my house and none of them have ever "soiled the throne." Is it something you do when you're in public to show dominance?

I mean, I know why a lot of guys piss on the toilet seat...because they're too fuckin stupid to pick up the seat. See ladies? Very simple reason.

You know what I wanna do to these assholes? And I know a few. If I die before them, I want them in my Will. Then I want them to travel thousands of miles to the reading of that Will, with thoughts of millions of dollars slapping them in their faces. I want my lawyer to say, "To my dear friend, Frank, whom I think of as a brother but who constantly pissed on my toilet seat during every party I ever threw, I bequeath one long, boney middle finger (which my lawyer delivers) and these parting words: 'Lift up the seat, you asshole!' "

———

Time really does fly. First it was just years, then it was decades. Of course, I'm smoking better weed now, so it might be all relevant.

Even days blur by. One morning, I woke up, took my morning crap, and when I came out, dinner was on the table. I mean, it was a big crap. I might have taken a nap after delivering that one. I remember the next couple days, I was walking funny. Like a part of me was missing.

If there's a way to know when something like that is going to leave your body, you can make serious money.

Go into a bar with a scale and bet the folks in there that you can lose 10 pounds in 10 minutes. Three 'ouchies' and a dozen flushes later, you can be a rich man.

I say "man" because it disgusts me to think of a woman doing that. That's a little bit too much redneck trucker trash for me. There's certain old fashion traditions I still appreciate. Like if your woman has to fart, she'll drive to the next state to do it. Common courtesy, right?

That's not sexist. I make fun of women and men. Watch ladies how easy it is to mock men. It's very easy. Tonight, when you go home, ask him how long his pinga is. He will tell you. He'll lie like a motherfucker, but he'll tell you.

And then ask him how he knows. He is not ashamed to say that he uses a tape measure. There might even be one on his dresser right now. If there is, look around and you might find some pills you can't identify. (Unless he left them in the little brown envelope they came in.) Oh, look, they came with a guarantee: "You will gain 3 inches or your money back."

Do you really think you're gonna get your money back? If they force you to take them to court, are you really willing to take it that far?

I don't really see women worrying about whether or not they're "deep enough." Walking around with a yardstick saying, "I'm good for about 13 inches, do I have any takers?"

Those pills they use to get people off cigarettes, fill them with nicotine so they can't get off them.

People love pills, you see the commercials. "So to fix your nasty, stuffy nose, try new Linablo." Then a dark, fast voice comes on, "May cause lesions, colic, balding, crabs, particle paralysis, blinding, deafness, projectile vomiting, and/or projectile diarrhea, the immediate melting of your soul, or one of your great grandchildren will be born with a third butt cheek."

I thought of a few more things you should never say to a cop when you get pulled over:

"You are so stupid." It may be true, but you don't need to point it out. He probably already knows.

"How did you become a cop?" That's no good. You never know, he might have crapped out as a pro basketball player but swings a mean nightstick.

One thing you do not want a cop saying to you: "I'm just gonna flip off the dashboard cam for a couple minutes…I'll be right back."

"Did you take a corresponding course?" Don't use big words like that. If he don't know what that means, he might think you mean he sucked pinga until a badge came flying out of the freakin thing.

Actually, all three of them go together pretty well. So if you're in need of a good ass kicking, there you go.

"Well, you have white powder under your nose too. Why should I believe your white powder is donut dust, Officer, when you didn't believe it when I said it?" That's a bad one. Once drugs get involved then you open yourself up to a cavity search. That is something you won't forget.

Question: What do they do if they find something up there? If it's one finger, all he can do is kind of stab at it. That does not sound good.

Neither does sending in another finger to kind of chopstick it.

Maybe they play the waiting game. To speed it up, they probably shove a suppository up you and some laxative down you. You can squeeze your colon as tight as you want, but as soon as you tire, it's gonna blow. The only thing you can do is try and shoot it out an open window.

I can see when a cop decides it's just not worth it. Do you really wanna walk down 3 flights of stairs and then look in a bunch of crap-covered hedges for a $20 bag of crap-covered cocaine? No, I do not.

Or what if he spins around and splatters you and your buddy? By the time you figure out why this guy's mooning you, you already took a first blast to the face. "Fuck! I ate a piece. I am going to fucking kill you."

————

The #5 phrase not to say to a cop is so obvious. And any guy that's been caught speeding would think this later on, but never say it. "I was speeding because your mother called and asked me to come over to bang her while your dad is at the bar." You better be wearing your Taser proof underwear at this point.

————

I got a big fat "maybe" by the Webster dictionary people that my word, Conglomafux, might be in next year's edition. How cool would it be to have your own word in the dictionary? And such a fantastic word. I mean, how would you like to be known as the guy that put the word "pud" in the dictionary? He's probably a pud, right?

It's a funny word in that the first time you hear it, you form an opinion in your head about what it means, and 97% of you are correct. To the other 3% I say, put the pipe down and get a breath of fresh air. If you're not sure, it means "a big pile of fuck." I'm sure the dictionary people will soften that up just a bit.

I'm sure pud has a really interesting definition, officially. I think if the Webster folks have a sense of humor, for pud's definition, instead of words, they will put a little mirror on the page beside it. If you have so much time to waste to find a dictionary and look up pud just so you can have the exact meaning at your fingertips…guess what? Yup. Pud.

People that do that are so pompous. They want to know the meaning of big 10 letter words to fit in with the rich people, and the little 3 letter words for the poor folks.

Just when the nation starts to think about getting in shape and chopping back some weight, they finally start legalizing pot. Believe me, I'm all for it. If you know me at all, you know I love pot more than any woman I've had so far. No offense.

This tiny little problem I see with the nation having the munchies is that fast food restaurants would be the new gold mines.

Soon, the day will come when you can walk into Burger King and ask for a Whopper covered with little marshmallows and hot fudge. They can call it the "Maui Wowee Whopper" and they don't even ask you if you want French fries; this fact is just assumed.

This may be something you might hear inside your favorite pizza joint one day: "Ok, I'll take 2 slices with Jujubes, a cheesesteak covered in tacos, one deep fried Italian hoagie, and large fries with La Brea Tar Pit Chili. Oh, and a Diet Coke. Honey, do you want anything?"

And gyms will become a place where all Chili dog eating contests are held.

"Welcome folks, please just hang your jackets on the treadmills just like you do at home."

I had a situation a couple days ago that required an immediate response, and since I didn't know what to do, I just want with a standard snap response: "Fuck no."

At the time, it seemed like the perfect response. Now, a few days later, I'm not so sure.

This is what happened.

I was throwing this Wingding (or was it a Hootenanny?) Anyway...it was a party. And a buddy of mine asked if he could bring his dad; he was a fan of mine...was.

I said, "Sure, just keep him out of the coke room...coat room." Holy crap, what kind of slip would you call that?

So the party's in high gear and so am I. I'm in the kitchen mixing myself another blackjack and I happen to look out the window. On the sidewalk, this old man is strolling and he suddenly stops. Then he arched back and sneezed into his bare hands.

I am grossed out. I turn away and start working my drink over. A few minutes later, I head out to the party. My friend runs over to me and says, "Buff, this is my dad." And he spins around this derelict with the 'Typhoid Mary' handshake.

'Mary,' his dad, says, "You are Buffalo Morgan. I am so glad to meet you." Then, like a bad 80's movie, everything went into slow motion. And here comes his green and yellow stained, who-the-fuck-knows-what-else-he's-infected-with hand...slowly.

And I jumped back...slowly. When his hand came to the appropriate distance where it should stop, it stopped. I think the response he was expecting was that now my hand should meet his hand to be shaken. This is about the time the "Fuck no" snap response popped out.

Now, I would love to say I followed it up with a brilliant explanation or joke, but I can't. Awkward silence followed. My brilliant explanation could have been, "I'm sick and don't want to get anyone else sick." But the words came 20 minutes too late.

I really hate losing fans like that.

All night, he's telling stories about WWII and about being in the Navy.

So the little voice in my head starts challenging me, "Go ahead, Buff, make a semen joke. I'll bet he guts you like a fish." And I'm like, "Shut the fuck up."

Eventually I left. Seemed like the smart thing to do at the time. Yes, I'm weak.

But really, what does Emily Post say to do?

I wrote my first song at age 7. It was a porno song, and it was highly plagiarized, set to a song/music I heard on Sesame Street. It kind of went like this:

"Rubber ducky, you're the one. I rub up against you 'til I cum. Rubber ducky, I have the twisted fantasies about you. Blo. Blo. Blo me OOO."

I bet I just wrecked that dumbass song for somebody.

My most embarrassing moment ever was when I was in Little League. I was the second baseman, and I didn't wear a cup. After all, what are the chances of a line drive hitting me in the balls? I tell you...2 to 1, at best.

First line drive and what happens? BOOM! Double play. Second line drive? Ca-runch!

My eyeballs spun like a slot machine. Before I knew what I was doing, I was pulling my pants down to inspect myself in front of 300 people. Thank god people didn't carry cameras around then like they do today. But I think all 300 of us can agree that my balls looked pretty mashed up. I felt like I was walking sideways for a month. Then one day, I woke up and there was no more pain. Man, I was so happy. And for the next couple days, I walked like some freakish emu protecting its last two eggs. Eventually, I stopped having nightmares and was fine. Fucking fine.

It's something how a line drive can hit your head, your stomach, or a leg three minutes later, and you're up and ready to play. The old cash register rings up a "No Sale." You could die; or worse, you could live. If it's a glancing blow, you'll be okay in 5 minutes.

This was a bulls-eye...or a homerun that caused a strike against me...or something. I didn't see it. If I would have, I would have caught it. It's the sound I'll always remember. Like punching wet cement: KAA...SPLAT.

I remember I was going to inspect my glove—you know, look for a hole—and my next thought came just a moment after I got my bell (balls) rung.

"Why does this not hurt? It seems like it should." Then things got a little fuzzy. By the time thoughts reached my inner voice, I think I went into shock. These are the thoughts I remember, like reading a telegraph line.

"Ok, here we go..."

"Alright, that's not too bad..."

"I can handle this."

Then my brain couldn't process what had happened fast enough. All of a sudden, I was a sentinel watching a monitor in the pain center of my brain. And I'm seeing a bunch of sticks on fire, running towards me. I was to understand these were nerve endings.

So now I'm surrounded by giant nerve endings, on fire, all yelling at me. So I start yelling back. It was about this time, I was back in reality…yelling. It felt like minutes, but it was probably about 2 seconds.

This is about the place in the story where the "Ball Inspection" comes in. I'm sure it was funny to someone…

———

Super Bowl 48…yeah, I don't do roman numerals…is being held in New York Giants stadium, currently called Metlife Stadium. Very exciting. I'm really looking forward to it. But it's not the game that has me. And it's not the commercials, though some are very good.

No, what has my attention this year is the interviews with the out-of-state drivers that are sure to be funny.

"What the fuck is Giants Stadium doing in Jersey? I drove around Manhattan for three days looking for the fucking thing. I was pissed the whole game."

Sorry, there's just too much shit in Manhattan to squeeze in a tiny 100,000 seat arena, and let me tell you "Big Apple city" people something: Before you get your suitcase full of money on Monday, about 50 New Jerseyians will be fondling that suitcase before we heave it into the river. It lightens with each caress…

Wouldn't that be just too cool if that little story started a huge scandal?

Even if we sent an E-check, they'd figure it out. "It's a lot less than I thought it would be. Why is it an E-check from 'Banko De Cayman'?"

"Yeah. We be just a buncha dumb hicks in the sticks of Jorsay."

Two words, folks…Tony Soprano."

One good thing about the computer age is that when you get advice from an old person, you can immediately check the facts on Google.

And soon, that medieval, toadstool-sucking advice can be wiped from the planet.

When I was a kid, my mom told me every time I got hurt, to let the dog lick the wound. Great advice, right?

Now, I knew if you got hurt, you needed antibiotics or penicillin. So as a confused kid, I thought when a dog licked himself, doctors scraped the dog's tongue, and that's how we got penicillin.

You might as well wrap your wound with gauze you found in a landfill.

But it is always fun when you can catch an oldster handing out bad advice. I got a scratch on my finger from a soup can. As I was telling this to a friend of mine, this old dude taps me on the shoulder and says, "You better go to the doctor or you'll get lockjaw."

And my mind said, "Get him."

So I said, "Ok, you old bastard, do you even know what lockjaw is?"

He just kind of blinked a quick 40 or 50 times. He seemed like he was in shock. I don't know if he was stroking out because I called him on something I was pretty sure he didn't know about, or because I called him an old bastard.

I am really getting tired of phone technology that just keeps adding little computer gizmo thingies. "Oh boy, another app."

How about adding things that people actually need, like a bottle opener. It's handy, and just think, if they would have thought of that back when they first started making phones, the bottle opener would be standard now.

How about a lighter? There are times I wish my phone had a lighter. Usually when I forgot my lighter. My phone could have a picture in my photo album of a lighter. And I could use that to really piss myself off for FORGETTING THE FREAKING LIGHTER AGAIN. Now that I smoke. You know. Tobacco. Yuck…

Now pot is a different story. There have been a few times I had a phone in my pocket but no lighter. And I notice this when I need a lighter and not a phone.

Although in the phone's defense, I have rolled joints off my phone, using it as a solid base. If I shocked a few of you, I'm sorry. And I don't roll joints anymore…I swear. My kids roll them for me. What? Why the hell else would I have kids?

Do you not see the wave coming that some states are making marijuana legal? I am so happy. And I think millions of us pot smokers share this beautiful thought: "It's about fucking time."

Even virgins are gonna love this stuff. Stress is worry and worry is unnecessary. This stuff makes stress float away. You may even think up a way to end your stress.

Know who really needs this stuff? People who protest abortion clinics. A couple hits of this and you'll see that what somebody needs to do is none of your fucking business and you should get a hobby.

Which reminds me…

I went to my doctor's office that happens to be in the same building as an abortion clinic. As I pulled into the parking lot, a bunch of the protesters came running over to my car. And they're yelling at me.

I don't have anyone in the car, so I yell back, "I'm here to get some blood work done." Then I smiled, "Thank god for places like this. Do you know how many kids I'd have running around this damn town if it wasn't for this fine establishment?"

And the race was on. I'd been wanting to break in my new sneakers and this was the perfect time.

All these people had one thing in common—besides obnoxious personalities and too much time on their hands. They were uggos. They either had way too many hard miles, or just God-given ugly. I think my comedy god, George Carlin, said it best, "Isn't it slightly ironic that people that are against abortion are people that you wouldn't want to fuck in the first place?"

R.I.P. George.

I ruined what would have surely been the greatest sexual experience of my life simply because I don't know when to shut up. It's just as well it didn't happen. It was gonna be much better for me than her. (Three minutes...tops.) She was so beautiful. But if she was as pure as she was trying to make herself out to be, she wouldn't know good sex from bad sex. She was a good Catholic girl...yummy.

As soon as I saw her, I asked her out...then I asked her name. I had to...she said yes. Suppose things had gone great and I proposed? How would that sound?

"Hey you! Wanna get married?" It just don't have a good ring to it…

Did you get it? Wedding…ring… I'm sorry, my brain don't get out much.

So for 6 sexless dates, I lied and bluffed my way through conversations all about the Bible. Finally, those improv classes paid off.

Date 7 is where I tripped at the finish line. When I picked her up, she greeted me with a kiss and wanted to go to a bar that served tequila.

She'd never had tequila and thought it sounded like fun.

This was the night it was gonna happen, until…

She was just beginning to slur her words when she asked me, "What is your opinion of Hell?"

So the "haha" funny side of me kicked in, "I don't mind marriage so as long as the bitch can cook." I even said it with a Swedish accent so she'd know I was kidding.

I looked into her eyes and I could tell the door had just slammed shut. She stopped with the tequilas and ordered some food. That is the international sign for: "You fucked it up."

Gone, man. It was never gonna happen. I could buy her dinners from then until the Eagles actually win a Super Bowl. That's a lot of dinners. Oh, and it still won't happen.

Just kidding Philadelphia fans. Put the snowballs down. Did you hear about that? During a parade, the fans threw snowballs at Santa. Apparently, not even Santa could deliver a championship to the Eagles, OOHHH.

Oh, sit down, drink your Schlitz and shut up.

I have a scientific question that requires incredible knowledge in the medical field that has, oddly enough, nothing to do with the genital area. Can somebody answer this?

Is there enough D.N.A. in a boogie to make that person or would it just make another boogie? I don't know, maybe somebody out there knows.

Alright, here's another question. If you were President of the United States, would you consider selling your bowel movements on E-Bay? I'm serious. I heard of people buying George Washington's hair clippings for like, a quarter million—dollars, not pesos.

Could you imagine what some nut would pay for that? Of course, it would sell. A fresh, stinky, presidential turd, mounted in a beautiful wooden display case. A little mirror on the back so you can see the other side.

And a little plaque of authenticity that tells the weight, time it arrived, and possibly a list of foods used in its creation.

I'll bet there are sickos out there that'd pay a million dollars for some "presidential poop." Patent pending, of course. If Obama starts now, he might be able to balance the budget by the time he leaves office.

He could also sell his hair on E-Bay every time he gets a haircut. And if you want hair, but not from his head, it gets more expensive the further down you go. A chest hair goes for 3 times a head hair; a pinga hair goes for 10 times more than that. If I was President…

By the time I would leave the Oval Office, all my hair would have been picked and packaged. I'd be hair-free everywhere my tweezers could reach. And I'd retire to my Hawaiian island I bought with the profits.

My hair will grow back. And the turds? Well, I was just gonna flush them anyway.

When I'm hungry any conversation I get involved in will eventually turn to food. Like last week, when I was talking to my mechanic…

"Mr. Morgan, you need a new carborator."

"Can you fix it, Luigi?"

Hey, my imaginary mechanics are all named Luigi. He needs the work.

"Sure, Mr. Morgan. Iya willa fix it righta nowa." And Italian.

"Great. Is there a buffet within walking distance Luigi?" Yeah, well fuck you.

"Thank you, Luigi."

Even with women it happens. Sometimes I can make it work to my advantage. One of my ex's loved sex 5 times a day, or more, in the same day. What a whore, right? God, I loved her.

So anyway, she signals me to the bedroom. I was on my way to the fridge. Long story short, I covered her in dark chocolate pudding and licked it off. It became our thing…twice a day.

Now I get all "horned out" when I eat dark chocolate pudding. And I'll eat it anywhere. I got some really nasty looks when I left church last week. Well, my slacks were at, uh, full mast. I was a little embarrassed. And when I get a little embarrassed, my brain doesn't function properly. And when my brain doesn't function properly, I have a tendency to say the wrong thing. In this case, I said, "Well, he kept talking about the virgin Mary."

Not good.

300 years ago, I probably would have been stoned to death.

Hey, in an alternate universe "stoned to death" sounds pretty cool. Is that like O.D.ing? How about "rocked to death?" No, in another universe, that sounds pretty cool, too.

———

Let's talk about death for a moment. 10,000 years ago, if you wanted to kill someone, you waited until your enemy went to sleep, then you dropped a rock on his head.

Now today, you shoot someone. Bullets are lead. Lead is rock. We haven't evolved at all.

Stabbing? It's metal…it's a rock. Chevy? It's metal…it's a rock. Piano wire? You know.

Well, I think they've completely done it. Every day of the year has a holiday attached to it. You have your secretary's step father day. Your do-it-in-the-dirt day. And I think July 3rd is drink-til-you-vomit day. It's a warm up for the Fourth of July.

We have about 10 real holidays, and half of them I don't know why they exist.

Like New Year's Eve. "I'm hanging a new calendar tonight, let's go out and get shit faced." I get excited when I see my first shiny penny of the New Year in about April.

Arbor Day. I don't even know what that means. Are we supposed to like, smoke leaves or something?

Groundhog Day.

If the groundhog sees its shadow, there's 6 more weeks of winter. No, if the sun's out, he'll see his shadow. And if you know how to read the calendar you hung on New Year's Eve before you got shit faced, there's 6 more weeks of winter starting February 2nd. Duh.

Valentine's Day is a beautiful day when you're in love. It's a lousy day if you're alone or married. I'm kidding, marriage is great...I guess. I'm sorry, I have to say marriage is great. It's part of my community service. I was protesting a church that still performed marriage services. It was the anniversary of my divorce and I got all fucked up and thought I'd be funny...you know, ha-ha, I'm a comedian. Apparently, there's laws against that sort of behavior. Who knew, right?

———

Do you ever notice how your sex residue...I mean, your kid, can ever get you through your childishness as they get older?

Like from years 0-2. All three of you are sitting around watching TV when a commercial comes on; the wife gets up to pee and, when she leaves the room, you crack a fart that wins awards. The kind that makes Tiquania turn its head, and say, "What the fuck, senor?"

And when the wife comes back, she walks right into it like a glass door. Stopped the bitch in her tracks, it did. Then she looks at you and what do you do? You point to the kid and say, "I think the little bastard shit himself."

And guys, here's a little tip: If she comes back in with the baby in less than 30 seconds and she's glaring at you, she's figured it out. Babies do not let off farts that only chili and Budweiser can produce until the ages of 6 or 7.

Between the ages of 2 and 4 is a good age bracket. Back then, I had 2 huge stacks of these bulky monstrosities they called V.H.S. tapes. I don't even know what V.H.S. means, but I had a lot of tapes of my favorite cartoons; my kids loved watching them as much as I did. I had 5 restaurants on speed dial. Some weekends, we'd have Bugs Bunny/Speed Racer marathons and, in the middle of it, we'd have 3 taco deliveries. God, I was such a cool dad.

Those parties were reserved for Saturday nights only. The couple times we did it on Sunday, they'd start complaining. You know, the little things kids love to bitch about... "Dad, I got school in 2 hours...I wanna go to bed."

"But the next one is Foghorn Leghorn." Damn lightweights.

And you know when the ship hits the iceberg on this one, right? One time, you'll be at the dinner table and one of your little tax deductions will say, "Dad, can we watch the Power Rangers later?"

"What the fuck is a Power Ranger?" You've lost your hold on the child. It now respects the cool kindergartener wearing the Punisher T-shirt.

From ages 5 to 10 is probably the best. Parenting is easy. Its parents that screw it up.

Here are two free tips on raising kids:

Any chore you give them, turn it into a game. Do you want the kitty litter box cleaned? Hey, it's a game. "Who wants to pan for gold? I think I see some huge nuggets."

I had a chart with my kid's names on it. Whoever got 25 points first got a Slurpee, but I only gave them 5 minutes to drink it. Nothing funnier than a child with a massive brain freeze. It also teaches them about gluttony. See? Smart. Now that's good parenting.

I know right when they figured out it was all just bullshit. For a couple days, nobody was panning for gold. And apparently, the cat had no room for this really big turd. So she twisted it out in my coffee cup.

I was stunned; it was a fresh cup. I was like, "What the fuck?"

The silver lining to this cute story is, I'm glad she did it in front of me. It was completely submerged. I thank God, because finding a cat turd in your coffee after drinking half of it could upset your day. Even if the coffee tasted a little funny, I'd drink it…until…you know, I struck gold. Coffee, like beer, you don't throw out…unless your cat shits in it…then you can.

That's tip 1A: "Don't eat or drink anything your cat defecates in."

Tip 2: Embrace bribing your kids. It's a win-win, screw your morals. "Billy, find the remote and I'll give you a quarter." Kids love quarters, so keep a roll on you.

"Billy, get Dad a quarter for a beer…I mean, a beer for a quarter. Billy, answer the phone and tell the nice bill collector your daddy's in the shower. Here's a quarter."

"Billy, shut the hell up. Here's a quarter."

I do not argue with positive results.

The teen years were tough. Everything was an argument. I tried reverse psychology, reverse/reverse psychology, and know what worked best? Pot. No, not for them, for me.

They become cauldrons of bubbling hormones in their teens. They know everything and want to bang everything.

"If you need me, I'll be over here watching Ren and Stimpy eating a pizza like a giant taco."

17 to 21 is also a good age bracket. I have my very own designated drivers. "Come on kids, let's go to the bar. I'll let you smell all the beer and vodka you can stand."

Here's a joke…kinda. What do you get when you call your son at 2 a.m., drunk in a bar, and he picks you up and takes you home and then you offer him a quarter? You get a son that says, "Go fuck yourself." A quarter don't buy what it used to.

Now come the exciting years… Marriage…grandkids…divorce. The bride's family still pays for the wedding, right? And what is the proper number of drinks the groom's father should have? Is it like 2…or 2 an hour? Either way, I'm not gonna be happy. I like to get into a rhythm with a slow steady buzz. It's like staying right in the middle of "maybe I shouldn't drive" and watching a tape of the event afterward, and saying, "oh, so that's why nobody was talking to me." Right there in the middle and I'm beautiful.

Like I said, "I'm glad I don't have to pay for this shindig." I'd be trying to get a loan from the blood bank. Say, how many gallons of blood do you need to cover this?

I'll bet that there's at least one person here tonight that learned how to French kiss by practicing with a dog. Not an ugly person, but a real dog. So fess up. Who was it?

I can see a dog really getting into it, by the way. Three seconds in and it'll jam that 2 foot long tongue down your esophagus and into your chest cavity.

It's true, dogs have really long tongues. I knew a dog that had bad arthritis in his back. He could barely bend over. But every day, he had corkscrew and nuts for lunch. I would have filmed it if I was just a little bit more of a degenerate…sorry.

Making love to your better half and being in love with that person is the best, isn't it? I had it like that a few times. Ironically, I had money both those times. Man, they were bitches.

But don't underestimate how good it feels to have sex with people you don't like. And for all kinds of reasons. Here are some of mine...and don't judge me.

One time, in my youth, I had sex with 2 women I did not know, within 2 hours of each other. It gets worse. I was trying to nail a dozen different women in one week, and I was 2 women short. I had 10 women friends that would let me get that close to them. I was so close, I was behind them.

So I was stuck on ten. The last day of the week, I hit a bar for a liquid lunch. And there sat this train wreck. She was so hammered, she didn't notice that I was watching her watch me in the mirror. Her head bobbing on the straw...she was so much in heat, I thought I might get number 11 in the parking lot. Then a flashing thought of sticking her with the bill appeared; you know, just a thought.

Well, we did "stank it up" in my car. When we were done, I told her I'd meet her inside, I had to make an important phone call. Soon as the door closed, I was gone…and I stuck her with the bill. Hey, I don't think she was trying hard is all. And that's my excuse. Moving on…

Number 12 was a complete mistake. Not to mention, I was under pressure to nail this chick by midnight. If I wasn't, you know, slappity-slapping her by midnight, the record would remain 11. I won't lie to myself.

So I ran home and jumped in the shower (I lost the coin toss. I was just going to hit another bar but then I thought that would be a real whore-like thing to do. And that's where the coin comes in.)

So I hit the next club and I see a cutie pie sitting by herself. I slither on over and buy her a drink. Over the next 20 minutes I get this chick's whole life story. And it's sad, man. I don't know how this girl hasn't blown her own brains out after hearing such a horrible life story. I almost wanted to cut her wrists for her.

And my pinga went from a mighty oak to noodle-like sapling. Nothing was getting that bird to fly that night, until she said, "And I haven't had sex in 10 years."

BINGO, honey. You just woke the freaking dead.

Things went just as planned. The only minor problem with scoring is that we started before midnight but finished after. I'm still counting it. We were "in" the act before midnight. You can debate me but I think I got this one.

Know what? Reliving that story with you guys really made me think. I really was a dirty rotten whore.

And here it is about 25 years after those days and I'm still not proud of it. I hope by the time they put me in the old folk's home, I will be proud. I don't want some old prude for a roommate, though. Here's how that conversation will go:

Me: "So how many lovers have you had?"

Lameo: "Well, let's see…uh, 3."

Me: "3? In one day? We have something in common already."

Lameo: "No…no; 3 in my life."

Me: "Ohhh…gotcha… Well, let me know if you need help cutting your wrists later."

I would like to clear up one piece of male bullshit that won't happen even though guys say otherwise. If you ask your average guy, "If you're on a plane and it's going down and you have three minutes to live, what would you do?"

You know what the average guy says? "I'm gonna bang the nearest stewardess."

Guess what? That is not going to happen. Your pinga is going to be hiding so far up your crotch, you will never see it again. He's hoping to survive the crash...even if you don't.

He'll eventually come out. Then he'll grab a piece of the fuselage and cut himself free. Then I guess he'll just join some porno circus and live the good life until he overdoses on a small mountain of cocaine. That's the way to go out.

If I sound a little depressed, it's because I am. A good friend of mine just...just...fucked himself. I mean, we've all done it. And as devastating as it was, we all bounce back. Yes, this is all a metaphor. But my friend really hurt himself. And actually, his own mother helped him fuck himself. I wonder what the medical term for that is.

Anyway, he's driving to work one morning and his mother calls him all excited. "Did you play your normal cash 6 lottery numbers last night?"

"Yeah."

"2, 6, 11, 33, 37, 48?"

"Yeah."

"YOU WON! 5 MILLION DOLLARS!"

"OH MY GOD! THIS IS GREAT! Mom, I'll call you right back."

Ring, ring. "Hello boss, this is Phil. You are a waste of human life. I hope you die a painful, bloody death. Chupa my pinga, ya bastard."

Ring, ring. "Hey Momma, we're going out to celebrate today. But first, read me back those beautiful numbers." "2, 8, 17, 33, 39, 48."

"What? What was that? What the fuck did you just say? That's not what you said a minute ago. Wait a minute, what glasses do you have on?"

"Hey, you're right. These are my driving..." click. "Hello? Hello?"

Ring ring. "Good morning boss, my goofy friend swiped my phone earlier and has been making prank phone calls to all my friends. I see he also called you. What did he say?" click "Hello? Hello?"

He had been out of work three years waiting for a job like this to fall into his lap. And on his three week anniversary he didn't even spit on the tip. Just: "OOOWWW."

Know what I hate most about being an adult? I have to talk like one and say stupid shit like, "I love my job" and "great idea, boss!"

So every once in a while, I'll think of something I liked as a kid. Last week, it was what my favorite animal was. I'll bet you can guess it... That's right. It was a frog. Is there a cooler animal? Most start off as an egg. Then it breaks out as a fish. Then it sprouts legs and loses its tail.

And for you pieces of shit who think it's fun to kill them, I hope there's a special place in Hell where giant frogs with 5 foot pingas rape your rotten soul in the Jacuzzi of Fire.

Anyway, so I'm remembering as a kid that I wanted to be a frog. And I'd be a tough frog, too. I'd learn to fight. And when I got good enough, I'd fight garter snakes.

How cool would that be? Jump out of a tree on to the back of an unsuspecting snake. Left arm has him in a choke hold. Right arm, hand in the first position, wailing away on the snake's right eye. Snakes can't close their eyes so he's forced to watch my little green fist pound the hell out of him.

And then I let it go. Let it go back to the hole, all fucked up. Probably have nightmares for a month. In my swamp, if you're a snake, I turn you into a vegetarian.

"Get away from my lily pad, asshole. Strawberries are to your left."

———

Is there anything more beautiful than a fresh tapestry of bullshit? And it will never end. Even after a nuclear holocaust, when there is only a million people left, someone will open a bar with a cute little slogan attached to it: "Get Bombed at Lovie's."

Advertisers are always looking for some mind dulling slogan that is "Hip and Today." The one that's gnawing at my soul recently is, "Certified Pre-Owned Used Cars."

Really? The car has 54,000 miles on it, that's not all test drives. Do you mean it's a pre-owned used car? And you got a knucklehead in a worse suit than yours standing behind you ready to certify that it's a "used car." I think I can figure out that the car is "used" on my own. I'm from Jersey, we're pretty good with that whole "figgerin" thing. Yeah, we be smot.

Thank you... Thank you... Wow...a little different than last weekend where I played. That was the "Detroit Afro-American Comedy Extravaganza and Gun Club." Or, at least that's what was spray-painted on the bed sheet outside. Could have been a crack house, I don't know. I mean, it looked like a house and we were... Ohhh. I mean, they were smoking crack.

As soon as I saw them smoking crack at the tables, I said to myself, "This is going to be an interesting gig." And it was. After the show they offered to pay me in weed. Yeah...I offered to accept it.

But don't worry, I didn't forget about you folks. (Throw a bunch of joints into the crowd.) You guys smoke? I mean weed. I love weed. I love whiskey and I love women. Three things that can fuck my life up and they all begin with W.

It's coming people. Weed will be legal soon. Can I get an Amen...again?

I can't wait. Anybody wanna do a road trip to Colorado tonight? We'll have to use your car. All the tires on my car live on a daily diet of Fix-A-Flat and the engine has more "stop-leak" then actual oil flowing through it.

Soooo…you drive.

It's not like I can't get good weed around here; heck, no. I just want to walk the aisles of a little store, with a little shopping cart, looking at properly sealed packages and not baggies. Ok, a big shopping cart. A monster truck sized shopping cart. "Aahh, give me a ton of that and a bale of this, please. I drove 1000 miles for weed and I want it all."

I do like weed better than alcohol. It's the whole sleep thing. After a night of drink, I always wake up after only an hour to pee, then I can't sleep…unless I smoke some weed.

There is one thing I really do like about drinking. You know that first time of the night when you realize you haven't peed for a long time and you think now might be a good time? And for just 10 minutes you empty your body. It's almost as good as sex. And in certain cases…

Guys can also adjust the flow…can women? Just curious.

We can adjust the pressure, too. It goes from water fountain mode to sand blaster in seconds. I found that little piece of talent when I almost feel asleep at a urinal.

I'm rocking back and forth and I realize I've been peeing for like, 10 minutes. So I kicked it into high gear to finish. That's when I realized I could clean off stains and chip porcelain. And don't underestimate a powerful urine stream. Under the right circumstances, it could be a hell of a weapon.

Suppose you find yourself in a fight and you don't know how to fight. And your application for a license to carry a concealed weapon is still on your desk because you forgot to pick up stamps. And the fist your opponent is making looks like a Miata. Isn't there something more you'd like to do other than crap your pants?

Well, pull down your pants and grab your, whatever you call it. I'll stick with pinga. A lot of guys name it. WHY?

"I call it the rock because…"

"Yeah, yeah, shut the fuck up."

That was the last time I was in a fight. He started walking towards me, so I pulled down my pants and grabbed my pinga.

Stopped this dude dead in his tracks. He dropped his fist and his jaw. I went for his jaw; I got his jaw.

Once those first couple drops of urine trickled down his throat, I believe his immediate goals changed. He seemed pretty desperate to extract my urine from his throat, and I don't blame him. I had asparagus for lunch…yummy.

He left after that. I guess I would, too. Anybody that would be willing to expose their pinga and pee on an individual are pretty much capable of anything.

The last couple years have been pretty crazy. Working every night...still not getting recognized. What's up with that? I mean, I've really been whoring myself. I did an hour gig for a set of medium grade, second hand snow tires. That's the last Jiffy Lube I do, I can tell you that.

But next month is gonna change all that. Hold on to your seats, or the seat of another if it's a better one than yours. I'll be releasing my "Buffalo Morgan/Betty White sex tape in 3D." Hey, don't judge. And for an older woman, she makes pretty good use of a king sized bed. I mean, she was everywhere. I didn't think 3D would work but, damn, I looked pretty good...except in this one scene. I don't know what was worse, my skinny Irish ass coming around towards the camera or her wrinkly ass coming at the camera.

I hope it didn't ruin her career. Couldn't hurt mine...nothing could. And before you ask, yes, I took Viagra that night. And yes, more than one. It was a small handful, really. Hey, when she showed me an old tattoo under her right boob was hieroglyphics, I sucked in those little blue miracles like Chicklets. I had to, once I saw "the whole package" my pinga said, "No fucking way." As soon as the Chicklets kicked in, he was like, "Ok, let's make those minor changes to your Will, then hammer you into the next world and me into early retirement."

No, go…that crazy bitch can take it. She must get porked by every guy that says hello to her.

Well, you guys can watch it and see. Oh, and she does this crazy thing with her tongue. See if you can get your lover to do it. It's pretty freaking cool.

As you can see, I'm pretty freaking busy. Last time was the first time in 2 years I went to a building where you buy stuff…a store, right? I got a…that thing with wheels…yeah, a shopping cart. I ended up buying a couple shirts with buttons on them that go all the way up. It was very exciting. Ohhh, and they have collars. Like this guy in the audience tonight. His shirt…only, you know…cooler.

Ohhh, I want to show you something. (Pull down zipper and pull out a tie) It's stuck. (Pull harder) Hey now…oohh baby. (Now it's out) So good.

Actually, a tie joke was one of the first jokes I ever wrote. Long before I hit the stage. You wanna hear it?

Ok, two guys are talking about ties; their names are Jose and Josb. But this is not an ethnic joke, it's a tie joke…ok?

"Hey Jose, I don't like Mr. Tie but I like Mrs. Tie."

"Why is that, Josb?"

"She has a great rack."

Great rack? Fuck you, I was 7. It got me a shitload of laughs in detention.

Do you know why there are so many weight/gravity challenged people out there? Because dieting sucks.

I get mean just thinking about cutting back.

And it's usually my agent that puts me in that mood. He'll call me up, and say, "Hey Buff, you have an audition for a bit part in a movie next week. Are you in shape or are you the no willpower, ketchup sucking, beer guzzling, pizza a-la-mode chomping, fat fuck you usually are?"

"Uhhh."

"Got it. Ok, let's try it this way. Eat the suppositories and stick the laxatives up your ass and don't stop until you're pretty."

And for some reason, I like my agent. Total douche, but I like him.

My willpower does suck, though. I won't even be out of the first day of official breakfast airtime before I start getting obnoxious. "All I want is a little bowl of fucking Cocoa Puffs."

After that, I have my handlers chain me up in the cellar. My behavior will only get worse. If that's what it takes to keep the checks rolling in…so be it.

Unless one of your ancestors crapped out a bank a hundred years ago, you're someone's slave…I mean, employee. And you probably have pain relating to your job—carpel tunnel, shoulder pain, a bad back—so I don't mind listening to my stomach cursing my mom's existence for a couple weeks. It's you people that keep this country rolling. I just make fun of what's wrong with it. Salute!

I don't think that a man should cry…unless he happens to be on a diet.

I cried on a diet before. I'll admit it. I was watching a movie and a Wendy's commercial came on. The announcer says, "We just improved the Baconator."

And I said, "You can't improve the Baconator." Yes, I do talk to the TV when I'm hungry.

So then he says, "We've added more bacon, we've added more cheese, and we deep fry the son-of-a-bitch."

I might be paraphrasing a bit, but I'm also professing my undying love as I lick the burger on my TV screen, probably with some crazed homicidal smile on my lips.

Then he says, "Get one of these heart attack inducing grease balls from heaven before Saturday, or you'll miss out."

And a tear rolled down my cheek, knowing I wasn't allowed to have a carb until the following Wednesday. And this had to be about a thousand carbs in one little wrapper. I was sinking fast.

Blindly, I ran to the panic button. I didn't want to push it but I did. And I hated myself for it. The panic button rings and an alarm at my handlers' homes screams out, and they race back to my house to double up on my chains. I am already plotting my escape. I may curse them…I may spit on them and, yes, even piss on them. They know not to listen to me and just get the chains on. And when they go, I shall weep some more. I do not diet with grace and dignity. It's more like threats and tantrums.

I know, I'm a baby. Sometimes, I hallucinate. Bob, one of my handlers, came to check on me. Probably to see if I had hung myself yet. Yeah, I get paranoid, too.

So, I thought I could hypnotize Bob. I looked him dead in the eyes, and said, "Bob, I will give you a thousand dollars for a pizza...any pizza...even the ones I mock in my act." Greasy Frisbees, I call them.

He just gave me the finger and left. So for the next 6 hours, instead of plotting my escape, I now tried to plant a brain tumor in his head with the power of my mind.

I diet poorly...very, very poorly.

––––––

Mona Lisa looks like just another chubby Italian chick. Yup, just another Snooki.

"Mr. Sagan. Mr. Sagan. Is it true that because there is no gravity on the moon, if I spank the chicken and point it at the Earth, I could hit someone in the head with it?"

Carl: "Once you figure the trajectory using the 5 ½ years, give or take a week, that it would need to travel that distance, figuring 20 feet a second and the angle at which re-entry is so important, so it doesn't burn up in our atmosphere, I would have to say…no. Do you even have a ticket for this event? Then get the fuck out."

When a woman don't want to get laid, she says she has a headache. When a guy don't want to get laid… What? It happens. Anyway, he says, "The best part of that blow job last night was the ten minutes of silence."

And if you are stupid enough to say that, you may want to sleep on your stomach that night. Men have lost pingas for far less than that. You know it's gonna be a bad day when your first job of the day is finding your pinga. I don't think you could make it the second job of the day. Unless you're calling the hospital. For me, that would be my second job. They're only gonna tell me to bring it with me anyway. Kind of useless going to the hospital without it.

Then they make you fill out a telephone book of medical questions about your life…present and past. Then hand you a Band-Aid wrapped in a $5000 invoice—a bill for all those services rendered.

———

Know what I would never want to watch? A sex change operation. Specifically, a guy getting changed into a woman.

A woman into a man? That's nothing. They superglue a piece of kielbasa to her coocoo, cut her hair and get her a dozen plaid shirts. DONE. It's also extra kind to get a subscription to Playboy for him/her for the first Christmas after.

But a guy...? Ugh. I don't want to think about it. I keep hearing a cleaver on a cutting board. Then a sinister voice say, "Ahhh, there it is."

Yuck!!! Let's go back to when the chick becomes a dude. So do you think this "new dude" will have an advantage in a singles bar? He would know the exact garbage a woman wants to hear so he can get laid.

The fat guy talking to me: "And just when I thought you were done and possibly sick, I saw your right butt cheek rise and you made some room in there, and emptied the restaurant…wow! Then you swallowed a pie…a whole freaking pie…in record time. I wish I had my stopwatch. And no utensils in sight."

I'm sitting there. But why…?

"Dude, it was like the food leaped out of your fingers and into your mouth. Like a planet being sucked into a black hole. Know what you did? Do ya? You turned gluttony into an art form."

I was stunned by his eye for detail and all I could say was, "Dude, you need to get laid. And if you can't find somebody, rent somebody. And don't worry, they don't charge by the pound."

I didn't care if I insulted him. I just wanted to leave. This dude was star struck. He wasn't listening to a thing I said. I could have said, "Well I worked up a good appetite giving it to your mom in the back seat. Not bad for $10. Which reminds me… Here, give this ten back to her. Tell her I said that was just a joke. I'm not really an international cut rate gigolo."

I gave him the $10. I'm not above bribery either.

Do you know that if you see a morbidly obese person staggering around, you're not allowed to call them fat? Not that they don't already know. I mean, if you take an unsliced whole pizza and fold it in half and eat it like a giant taco, you have a problem. I saw somebody do that one time… Huh, I think it was me.

I weighed over 300 pounds for a while. I knew how to maneuver around a refrigerator. And I always had this fear that whenever I was out in public, someone would call me on it…

"Hey man, you're fat."

"Thanks, I kinda know that. Yeah, I get it, I'm too short for my weight. I know, you're a fucking genius. Someday your intelligence is just gonna kick you right in the balls."

And as he's trying to figure out if he's supposed to be insulted or not, I walk away.

But I never got called on it.

Now I've called people on stuff, but not weight. It was over-intelligence. That's right, I will call someone stupid to their face, and I will recite the incident that has given me the opinion of why you are that stupid. It could be that I saw you fingering your bum because you couldn't figure out anything better to do at that moment.

Or you may actually say something and my opinion will be cast. "I hate moving my left hand from here to here. And that's why I don't use my turn signal, or masturbate with this hand."

So you see, I feel when another person makes such a broad statement like that in the middle of a conversation, you can get a court order for said offender to be fixed. We do not need infinite generations of what I call "muck." And if you know me at all, you've found out that means mental fuck.

And let's destroy all TVs. It's rotting our brains. Honey Boo Boo may be causing someone that has the potential to be a super genius one day to stagnate. That person can't escape the pathetic glow of a little fat kid farting…or whatever she does.

And that person may be the one who has or will develop a working time machine. And we can use the knowledge to go back in time to a world before women started shaving…you know…down there. HEY! Some of us prefer carpet to hardwood.

Do you know why guys don't do the shaving thing down there? Where would I start? How far up and how far down? From my belt line to the top of my thighs? Below my chest and down to my knees?

I can't imagine that look ever coming into style. Looks like if you were committed to the project, it would extend from the ole Adam's apple to the fuzz on your toes. I don't have that kind of time every day. If you do, I have three words of warning for you: Watch. The. Nipples.

If that was too much to follow, I can cut back to fat people, Honey Boo Boo, and nipples. Do you have the gist? Ok, moving on…

If men and women…

What? Sorry, women and men (bitch). If women and men are still doing that Mars/Venus thing, I think we should work on getting everybody back on Earth…bitch.

Now, a group of us men had a meeting last night and we feel that if we concede to some of your demands, and you concede to some of ours, it will definitely bring us all closer together.

Ok, according to the list you provided, your #1 complaint is us men leaving the toilet seat up. A valid complaint. As a veteran of throwing up into toilets, I concur that it is always better having the seat down. Everyone knows that all the deviate hairs congregate on the flat top of the porcelain. No matter what condition I'm in, that becomes the worst part of the night. So we will concede that one to you. Men will never lift the seat again. Our lawyers are working on the legal document as we speak. Now in return for this generous sacrifice, we would just like one small concession on the women's part. Men will have the freedom to pee in the tub, the sink, or the cat box.

If you need to take a vote on it, remember what we're giving up over here.

———

My dad always said, "Never punch a woman," and that was great advice...until I met wife #2. After the initial, "Good afternoon, Mr. Morgan, if there's anything I could do to make your stay here better, please let me know."

After that little speech I should have punched her square in the mouth. Because it was about this time the devouring of my soul had begun. And I was too stupid to know it.

She was my new agent in Chicago. She knew everything about me. Like my strengths...which are few. And my weaknesses...which are many. She touched on 2 of my biggest weaknesses with her next sentences. "By the way, I'm having an ounce of high grade marijuana delivered to your room later. And if you'd like,

I'll come up and roll it into joints for you. I roll an amazing joint."

Now that's the kind of statement that could get me thinking about marriage, or molestation, in the next few hours. But this crazy bitch did her homework. Every syllable had her 38 double D masterpiece of perfections, rising and falling at a hypnotic rate. Within an hour, I was dead. I floated behind her in the aroma of her presence. Looking back, there was a hint of sulfur. I should have realized that...20/20 hindsight.

My first red flag that I had fucked up my life yet again came a week after the wedding. I said, "Hey honey, can you roll us a joint before we go to bed?"

And do you know what the bitch said?

"Fuck you."

Whooooaaahhhh. That's when I knew I ruined my life...again. My first thought: "I hope she doesn't ask me for half the stuff I got from the first divorce..."

———

Ask anybody what creatures would survive in a nuclear holocaust, and they'll say either cockroaches or lawyers. No, I'm just kidding...kind of. No, they say cockroaches or rats. Two things most people have a problem with.

Why can't it be people and bacon? I mean, pigs. If I survive, I don't want to eat rats. Look how tiny the drumsticks are. Even the cockroach would be like, "You're kidding, right dude?"

And obviously the feast of cockroach soufflé isn't happening. I'll take a hatchet to the jugular long before then. There are candy makers out there that turn them into snacks. I've seen them made into taffies, deep fried, and chocolate covered. Know what I'd say to these people? "Fuck you." Cockroaches are the vilest creatures to scoot around on the linoleum floor.

I'd rather be mauled by the biggest bear in Jellystone Park. What? Oh…the biggest bear in Yellowstone Park, than have the smallest cockroach walk in my mouth while I'm sleeping. They're so dirty. I don't think they'd be any dirtier if a dog turd on the front lawn broke up into a hundred pieces and the pieces became cockroaches.

And you want to sprinkle them in powdered sugar? Well, fuck you.

Do you think the nuclear fallout could form hybrid creatures? Hybrid—this year's buzzword.

How about a cockroach rat? That even sounds nasty to say. Could you imagine trying to kill a half pound, white hair covered cockroach with your slipper? You might have to stomp it a couple dozen times. I could imagine they'd put up quite a fight. On second thought, you might just want to move.

———

A lot of people are dog people because they don't realize cats do funny things. We've all seen the videos; cats sliding across linoleum floors and walking into sliding glass doors. It's funny when people do it. It's funny when dogs do it. And it's even funnier when cats do it.

A cat seems to be funnier because they look more intelligent while doing it. You don't think it'd be stupid enough to do that, but they do it all the time.

My little pile of princess fur has done both of these stunts many times. It's like her memory card is full and new information is just deflected to the outer reaches of time and space. Not existing on the memory card is valuable information that includes wet floors and clean glass doors.

But cats are always fucking up. These are things she's done just in the past week, and I'm not there a lot, but this is what I've seen...

Sunday, I left my water glass unattended on the coffee table. When I came back with more salsa, there she was lapping up my water. As I walked towards her, she stopped. She just stood there, staring at the water inside, and then…she sneezed. And it was a good one.

She splashed water all up in her face. For the next three minutes, she went ballistic. She just ran and screamed throughout the house. Once I stopped laughing, I caught her with a huge fish net. She was wild. She must have some Tasmanian devil genes mixed up in there with her feline ancestors.

Can that happen? I flunked gene splicing in High School. But does that happen in the wild? One species banging another species just to get laid. Could my cat's great grandmother have been getting a drink in a stream when a Tasmanian devil came up to her and gave her what for? Sorry, I like that expression.

"Gonna give her what for." Very trailer parkish.

Ok, that was Sunday.

On Tuesday, I left my pot unattended on the table. By the time I paid the college educated graphic designer for the pizza he was delivering to me, my little princess nibbled down a little bud the size of a small rat. As I put the pizza on the coffee table, I kinda put it all together. She was still chewing; her mouth was a nice shade of green and she was staring at me. It was almost like she was putting her thoughts into my head. It sounded like, "I'm sorry dude, but is that pizza?"

So we split it.

Wednesday, I threw the fucking coffee table out. It just seemed like bad voodoo.

Friday, I had just gotten home and was sitting on the sofa. She was asleep on the dining room table. Her back was half an inch from one of the ledges. I'm ten feet away, watching her stretch out. Then...before I can move to her, she rolls over and straight off the edge. She landed on her outstretched legs and kind of bounced off her paws on to her side.

It hurt. I know it hurt, but she would not acknowledge it. In her mind, that is how she'd planned it. But it's flawed and she knows it.

As she was falling, we locked eyes for a second. My thought was, "You are so stupid."

Her response was, "Yup!"

You know that you are what you is, don't you? If you pump gas for a living, you're either a gas pumper or a Petroleum Distribution Technician, depending on your education.

Every day, the average person makes a thousand decisions about their futures— immediate or otherwise. Some are bad decisions.

And that brings me to my problem. I must have a Mother Theresa streak in me. Everybody likes to have a drink with me and then admit a horrible chunk of their past. I don't know why. They do know it might become part of my act so they put a disclaimer at the end of the story instead of at the front, where it may be considered.

If you're gonna rape my ear with an incredible story of something so fucked up that only a man of your mental stature could accomplish it, start the story with, "Hey Buff. I want to tell you something, but don't tell anyone." Do that, and I just might keep it to myself.

But if you tell me a story that ends with, "And that's how I got three generations of women in the same family pregnant." Yeah, your story will be on stage at the next gig. Your shit is my gold.

And some people get pissed off. I had one guy threaten to sue me. He was smashed, and he came over to me at the bar and just started in on how he used to have sex with his neighbor's cow three times a day for a year. Not the guy's wife, an actual moo-moo cow. He went into graphic detail and, when he was done, he said, "But don't tell anybody."

So I put my hand on his shoulder, looked him square in the eye, and said, "Fuck you."

Question: Suppose when you die and there is a great Creator (insert any name you want here), and it says, "Hey, let's watch the DVD of your life." When it comes to "those" scenes, what are you gonna say?

And that is why I only have sex with people. The DVD...? I have my share of bad scenes...just not "cow poker" bad.

I was asked to write a sitcom recently. A lot of people are really freaking tired of reality TV...REALLY FREAKING TIRED.

So I went to see the assistant to the Assistant Director. I think he doubled as a gopher there. He even brought coffee for the janitor's hooker wife. So I knew he wasn't exactly my ticket anywhere. So I just dazzled him with bullshit.

I'm in his office and I just start talking about whatever comes into my head. "Ok, a slick husband...he's always trying to get over on his dim wife who's always been out-foxing him and destroying his wacky plans. Is she just playing dumb? Nobody knows. So in the first episode, the husband is at work and one of his friends gives the husband a seed. One marijuana seed. So the husband takes it and sneaks out of work with it; his black friend looks into the camera and winks.

So anyway, he takes the seed home to his wife and tells her it's a tomato seed and he wants to grow a tomato plant from the beginning. She thinks that's so nice, so he lovingly plants it.

Then the narrator says, "4 months later."

It's a full grown plant with big buds on the ends. So the husband is massaging the plant and professing his love for it. Then he tells it that tomorrow night he has to destroy it. His voice is cracking because he really loves his pot plant. Tomorrow, he'll dry it and smoke it.

The wife hears the end of the conversation and how upset he is, so she decides she's gonna get rid of the plant herself. She still thinks it's a tomato plant and the "buds" just won't turn red.

So, you see, she wakes up early the next day and takes the plant outside, then comes back in and starts making breakfast.

Now the husband comes down the stairs. He goes into the kitchen and kisses his wife, "Good morning, honey." Then he swings his head to where the plant was, and says, "Good morning, Charlie. Charlie...?

WHERE THE FUCK IS CHARLIE???"

And the wife is shaking her head proudly. "Oh honey, I saw how much Charlie meant to you, so I got rid of him for you."

The husband says in a really high voice, "Where did you put him?"

As she points to the door, she says, "I put him outside."

The husband races to the door. Then the wife continues, "Luckily the trash men were going by so I gave it to them. They were thrilled. They said they love green tomatoes."

Then, you know, a little something different that no other sitcom is doing right now...special effects. Hah! We'll get the husband's head to float a couple inches off his neck and have steam come whistling out his ears.

Then he says his weekly catch phrase: "Bitch, I'm gonna kill you."

Then he chases her like, a dozen times, around the kitchen table...but fast, you know? Like on Monty Python. Ohh, we'll cue up some old Benny Hill music, too. You know, that chase stuff.

When I was done with my awesome idea, the Assistant Director only had one question. "Do you have a second episode?"

I was surprised by that, but the B.S. was still flowing. So I said, "Kind of. Basically the same shit, but the husband gets into making bathtub gin and the wife pulls the rubber stopper thinking it's her diaphragm."

Apparently I was wrong about this guy. He did have a lot of power. I am not allowed in the city of Cleveland anymore.

So if I remember right, that makes 5 cities, 3 districts, a couple of territories, and an island in the Bahamas. I forget which one, so I just avoid the Bahamas all together.

———

Life is full of highs and lows. Highs are better, of course...always. Nobody ever asks for more misfortune.

Highs make you scream, "Yeah!"

Lows make you scream, "Fuck!"

Don't you wish you could have one "do over" in life? Well, just get to a spot where you can pinpoint the exact moment in your life where you drove your future into the iceberg.

And yes, I do understand the ramifications of time travel and the problems it can create; I'm not an idiot.

I have rules on such subjects. I repeat, I am not an idiot.

Rule 1: You can only fix the problem right at that time. Whatever you fixed should be something that will never happen again, and don't do something like erase the first time you had a cigarette because now you're dying of cancer.

If you didn't start smoking that day, you probably would have started in the next couple of weeks. And that puts you right back into the oxygen tank.

Rule 2: You can't go back to hurt somebody. If you're a mob hitman, you can't go back to whack the target you missed last time because you had to stop and take a piss. So you botched the job and got your back broken. That's just tough shit; no flashback/time travel for you.

Rule 3: You can't go back for money. You can go back and make a better career choice, but you can't bet the mortgage that Buster Douglas beats Mike Tyson, or anything like that.

Rule 4: Once your request is processed and approved, you have one week to think about the changes and consequences to your present life if this particular event is altered.

If you're a parent and you want to change something in your childhood, you have to consider the children you have now might never be born. I'm sure that's a selling point to some.

Ohh, and one last thing about time travel. This point came up during an adult conversation I was having with another adult. And this knucklehead just couldn't see how he was wrong. Some people, am I right?

So he wants to go back and kill Hitler. So I said, "Dude, you're 58. Hitler died like 70 years ago. You were only a swimmer in your dad's marble bag. What were you gonna do? Slap Hitler in the face with your little tail? That would only annoy him, not kill him. So you cannot go back in time to before you were...let's say, ten."

Why not before you were ten? Because it's my game, my rules. And I don't want to play anymore.

I believe in a lot of weird, freaky things, just not time travel. But if I'm wrong, like I usually am, and one of you freaks...I mean, folks who are here tonight find out a way to travel, could you deal me a solid? Could you go back to

November 11, 1975, my junior high school, find me there and tell me to ask out Karen Lexinberg before lunch?

The way it happened was, I asked her out one and a half seconds before the lunch of tacos and the flu I didn't know I had, met up together in the same place. Yes, I pooped my pants in front of the girl I loved and/or lusted over. I never had a good day in school after that.

I'm pretty sure that is one of my defining moments that I'd like to alter. Roll those freaking dice.

―――――

I may be wrong saying this, but I don't think I am. People that can't cook should not be allowed to throw dinner parties unless it's being catered.

"Thanksgiving of '89." Everything at this couple's house was done...except the turkey. The first time our hostess pulled it out, it was as white as a drowned Irishman being pulled from the lake by moonlight.

"If we duct tape his head back on, we might be able to save its life." I might not had wanted to say that as loudly as I did...but I did.

So she glared at me, took the turkey out of the plastic bag, cranked the oven to 3000 degrees, and plied us with liquor.

———

Problems of the one night stand...and there are many. I will be using the most common problems sprinkled with personal stories. For all I know, they may be all about me. These come from the good ole days of being a black-out drunk and a perpetual male whore. Talk about a career path...

First, let's talk about fear.

Here's the situation. Your eyes are closed, your head is screaming, the mattress supporting your naked carcass is definitely not your own, and you're not sure if you want to know what's on the other side of your eyelids.

You may want to go for the gut reaction to know if this was a great night or are there dark cold clouds of dread. You won't find a reaction there. Your gut went on strike at 3 a.m. when we stumbled upon a 24-hour cheesesteak joint.

WAIT! That's an actual memory. But who was with me?

Trust me, once you fail with the "who," you'll finally crack one eye and take a look. For me, I always found it was one of two kinds of women lying there; a 1955 Betty White lookalike, or a 2014 Betty White lookalike, more the latter.

———

Hey! You know the old scary movies where someone opens a door and it creaks? That's what my eyes used to sound like.

My biggest fear was having my eyes pop open to witness a dude on the other side of the bed with one eye open wearing a confused look on his face. I absolutely do not care what other folks do. I care what I do. I'd probably start the conversation like this:

"If you roofied my ass then you are not gonna enjoy today. There better be a woman behind me, beneath me, or on me that I can't see."

I think if that ever happened, my initial reaction would be, "Does my ass hurt?"

Sometimes you crack that eyelid and your face is planted in the back of the head of a Final net-abusing mystery girl. And you know she's a girl because you still have a handful of...hubba, hubba. Although now that doesn't prove Jack...or in this case, Jane.

Now you know you have to do a reach around to be completely sure. I don't want to feel any pinga...NONE! Not even a single one. All I wanna feel is space. Glorious, objectless space.

———

If I hit a tree trunk, I am not going to be happy. And after its owner leaves with it, I might just cry.

Once gender is established, then you have a moment that will take you to the polar opposites of your emotional spectrum. I usually start off on a very positive high, hoping for a Jessica Alba lookalike with low standards. A lifetime of love and lust with her is suppressed by a brilliant thought of rolling over and having sex with her for breakfast. Hurry up and snap a picture!

The first thought that Jessica Alba is a wildly unrealistic scenario comes from your breath. The only three flavors I could identify of the 50 or so floating around in my mouth were beer, bourbon, and Funyons. And we all know Ms. Alba isn't going to bang me after watching me dunk Funyons in a beer mug filled with bourbon.

Yup...here come the dark clouds.

ABOUT THE AUTHOR

My name is Barry Hemmerle. I was a bouncer at a comedy club in the mid 1980's. Before Tim Allen broke through, we hung out together and he suggested I take a stab at comedy. After my second show, the manager thought I was good enough to M.C.

Using the name Barry Von, I worked the east coast sharpening my style of sarcastic wit. Besides jokes, I'd occasionally break beer bottles over my head or let audience members rub a spot on my temple for good luck. {It's a bullet someone put there over the beating I gave him as a teen.

A SPECIAL THANK YOU TO YOU!

On behalf of everyone at Freedom Of Speech Publishing, thank you for choosing Buffalo Morgan's King Lomafux: Sick & Funny Comedy from Buffalo's Vegas Show for your reading enjoyment.

As an added bonus and special thank you, for purchasing Buffalo Morgan's King Lomafux: Sick & Funny Comedy from Buffalo's Vegas Show, you can enjoy discounts and special promotions on other Freedom of Speech Publishing products. Visit http://freedomofspeechpublishing.com/vip/ to learn more.

We are committed to providing you with the highest level of customer satisfaction possible. If for any reason you have questions or comments, we are delighted to hear from you. Email us at cs@freedomofspeechpublishing.com or visit our website at: http://freedomofspeechpublishing.com/contact-us-2/.

If you enjoyed Buffalo Morgan's King Lomafux: Sick & Funny Comedy from Buffalo's Vegas Show, visit www.freedomofspeechpublishing.com for a list of similar books or upcoming books.

Again, thank you for your patronage. We look forward to providing you more entertainment in the future.

Buffalo Morgan's King Lomafux

Sick & Funny Comedy from Buffalo's Vegas
Show
By Barry Hemmerle

Printed in the United States of America
The publisher offers discounts on this book when
ordered in bulk quantities. For more information,
contact Sales Department, Phone 815-290-9605,
Email:
sales@FreedomOfSpeechPublishing.com

Freedom of Speech Publishing, Leawood KS, 66224
www.FreedomOfSpeechPublishing.com

ISBN: 1-938634-16-0
ISBN-13: 978-1-938634-16-1